The Dark Circle

The Dark Circle

A BLACK MAGIC STORY

PAUL J. KEEBLE

Library of Congress Control Number:		2015918927
ISBN:	Hardcover	978-1-5144-6456-4
	Softcover	978-1-5144-6455-7
	eBook	978-1-5144-6454-0

To order additional copies of this book, contact:
Xlibris
800-056-3182
www.Xlibrispublishing.co.uk
Orders@Xlibrispublishing.co.uk
724462

CONTENTS

The Dark Circle is a black magic story by Paul J Keeble.

The author writes that he is a Pagan High Priest, having studied and practiced Pagan worship for over 30 years. He believes in several Gods & spirits and worships the Goddess. He believes in the beauty of nature and the care and preservation of all living things. The author has observed but never participated or assisted in black magick, worship or ritual. The author can only speak for himself and does not represent other pagans. However, neither he nor his close associates believe in Satan as a deity, believing that the evil comes from within us. However this evil can be born, nurtured and grown from our actions, our experiences and what we are exposed to in life. The author has had to heavily research the subject of black magick for over five years to enable him to write this book and from his findings he strongly advises that readers do not become involved in black magick or any of the black arts, as this type of participation can encourage the very evil that is personified by the symbol of Satan.

This book 'The Dark Circle' is the first book of a trilogy, by this author. The Dark Circle does conclude in a climax at the end and can therefore be read in isolation but the characters, relationships and challenges explode in a new and continuing story 'The Clash of the Circles'.

If the author had written a murder mystery it would not mean he approved of murder, likewise it must be said that the author does not agree with the views, beliefs or actions of Satanists. In the story the author has portrayed the Satanists as they see themselves, so neither the Satanists nor their actions are being justified by the author.

The views and opinions expressed in this book are expressed by the characters and are therefore not those of the author himself.

ACKNOWLEDGEMENTS

Without the love, support and encouragement of my family, Sandra my understanding and patient wife, Joshua and Matthew my wonderful sons, who were being continually told to be quiet as 'Daddy is writing', this book would never have been possible.

During my research I found that some of the written and documented information both in books and on the web was highly questionable and in certain cases totally inaccurate. However my research included the privilege of being invited to Satanic covens where I was able to talk to the members and observe some of their rituals and workings. Readers must remember that this detail was subjective and word of mouth and the story is totally fictional, so the information cannot be relied upon academically. Unlike most authors I am unable to give the names of these co-operative people as they have all insisted they remain anonymous, for obvious reasons. Nevertheless they know who they are and without their advice, guidance and information this novel could not have been written.

Paul J. Keeble

ILLUSTRATIONS

Sketches marked * are by Dannii. L, a valued friend and based upon the author's descriptions. All rights for the book and all future publications have been passed to the author.

Symbols & signs marked ** have been created digitally by the author with the assistance of his two sons Joshua & Matthew.

Images & pictures marked *** have been taken from Google search as they were labelled as 'for reuse commercially'.

CHAPTER 1

The Pinnacle

* A Griffin

Peter Houston really wasn't sure he was doing the right thing. In fact deep down he was almost sure he wasn't. However his life had been so unrewarding over the last two years he had to do something to change his luck. The Medium seemed convinced this group would improve his luck, even bring him power and wealth. It had to be worth a try, he was 31 yrs old and had absolutely no prospects. It was Friday evening, he had no date and he could always walk away if he didn't like it.

Peter lived in Brighton and responding to the invitation he was driving to a village called Bridlington. He had taken the A27 from Brighton and then at Polegate joined the A22 going north away from Eastbourne. He saw the sign to Stone Cross. He didn't have a sat nav but the man who had telephoned him had given him detailed directions. He found the cross roads with the big old Celtic cross (the cross with a circle at its centre) directly ahead in front of the church graveyard and the name of the town on a large sign on his left by the traffic lights. He was in the right place. He followed his instructions and turned left at the lights and drove up the country lane. He passed the pub on the left that advertised value for money carvery lunches and knew to take the next right. Sure enough the sign said Bridlington and as he came out the other side of the village he started to slow down looking for the large house. He found the sign "The Pinnacle" on the left and turned into the entrance of the driveway.

It wasn't at all what he was expecting. He had sussed this group was some form of religious cult, possibly even Satanic (hence his doubts and worries). So he was expecting a house that was from the 'Adams Family' or the 'Munsters' or from the set of a ghost story in a 1950s black and white film. What he was presented with, was a pair of beautiful ornate green metal gates that stood about twelve feet high. On the left and the right were two stone pillars from which the gates hung. Peter climbed out of his car and immediately saw that there were stone walls the same height as the gates on both sides of the entrance. He guessed the wall probably encircled the property. When he looked up he saw the pillars were about three feet shorter than the gates and wall, and that was because both pillars had an amazing sculpture of a griffin on the top. (The griffin has the head of an eagle and the body of a lion. Sir John Mandeville wrote about griffins in his 14th century book of travels that "A griffin is more strong than eight lions. For one griffin will bear, flying to his nest, a great horse". More significantly John Milton, in Paradise Lost II, refers to the legend of the griffin in describing Satan.) When Peter looked at the griffins he noticed that both griffins had eyes that didn't match and then to his shock he suddenly noticed that one of the eyes on each griffin was moving. As the shock passed he came to realise that the griffins were elaborate CCTV cameras. Although the gates were closed he could see through them as they were an open metal lattice and a wide sweeping driveway stretched ahead and curved towards what could only be described as a mansion. He found an intercom mounted on the right hand pillar. On request he announced his name and the gates started to swing open.

**An Inverted Pentagram

He climbed back into his car and drove slowly up the driveway noticing how the driveway didn't have a weed and the lawns either side were so trim they could be astro turf except the colour and sheen denoted the real thing. As he approached the house the driveway opened out into a large circle with parking behind, and in the middle stood a pond with a fountain, but what a fountain. It was a statue of a young woman that poured water from a jug under her arm, but the statue was spectacular. The girl looked real, alive. He expected her to turn towards him as he circled the pond and looked for parking. In the parking areas behind the pond and either side of the entrance steps there were about twenty cars parked. Peter wasn't normally ashamed of his little five year old Vauxhall Corsa but it seemed very out of place here. With one exception all the parked cars were recent models of very expensive cars. They included two new Jaguars, a Porche and an Aston Martin. The exception was a small white Suzuki parked at the end. He found a space, parked up and as he got out the car the cold reminded him it was now December. He could see his breath as he made his way up the steps towards a pair of imposing large wooden entrance doors.

Before he even reached the doors they started to slowly and silently open inwards and a man appeared in the arched entrance. Peter felt uneasy as the man was tall and looked down on him as Peter climbed the last few steps. The man was probably in his sixties with short but distinguished silver hair. He was dressed casually but wore an expensive purple shirt and a silk cravat around his neck. He would have looked at home walking into the bar at St. Andrews Golf Club. He held out his hand, "You must be Peter" he said "Can I take your coat?" As Peter removed and passed his coat to him he knew he hadn't met him but he recognised the deep rich voice of the man who had telephoned him and invited him to meet his friends. He passed Peter's coat to a waiting servant. "Welcome to my home, please come in. My name is Aleister." He stepped back and ushered Peter in through the entrance.

The entrance hall that greeted Peter was large and grand. The hall was circular and had two staircases, one on the far left and the other on the far right. They curved inwards and upwards in a semi circle to meet the two ends of a balcony. At the centre of the balcony was a large pentagram, a five pointed star that looked down on the guests arriving. A pentagram is usually shown with the single point upwards in most pagan environments. Here however, it was shown with the single point downward. This meant there were two points at the top of the pentagram and this often signifies Satan. The two points are representing the horns of the Goat of Mendes also known as Baphomet. Although it didn't make sense to have two staircases going to the same place, it looked totally right, balancing the amazing effect of the hall. There was a sweet smell in the air that Peter couldn't place, like violets but not violets. A few guests were still in the hall greeting each-other as they slowly made their way through another double door on the right. "This is only a meeting not a celebration Peter, but the meeting itself is for members only, so I am afraid I will have to ask you to leave, when we are ready to start our meeting. However I wanted to meet you and introduce some of my friends."

As Aleister spoke he led Peter through into a large room that had tables on the right with drinks and canapés. As the guests were chatting to each-other three aproned servants were offering drinks and snacks. Peter noticed another symbol on the wall above the drinks table. It was another pentagram but larger and ornate. It was a black circular plate with a white circle drawn near the edge and the five pointed star or pentacle inside the circle, was inverted, as before. However this time a goats head was drawn inside the pointed star and strange symbols were drawn on the edge of the plate, outside the white circle. Peter didn't recognise it but it was The Sigil of Baphomet, the official insignia of the Church of Satan. Peter did nevertheless find it un-nerving.

Aleister led Peter towards a stunning young lady who was standing on her own and dressed as though she was going to the proms. Peter guessed she was about twenty five. She wore a beautiful figure hugging cream dress that nearly touched the floor. Her blond hair hung down to her shoulders and her eyes were a mesmerising blue. "This is Caroline, likes to be called Carrie" Aleister said. "We only use first names here and if you are fortunate enough to be invited to be a member, you will be allocated a new name. Privacy is very important to us all." Aleister turned and looked at Carrie, "This is Peter, Carrie, he is just visiting to meet some of our friends. Will you look after him, I need to make arrangements for our meeting?" "Of course I will" Carrie said. At that Aleister turned and walked away, back to the hall. Carrie looked at Peter, "This is your first time here then?" "I haven't actually met Aleister before." Peter said. "After my Mum died I missed her so terribly I agreed to see a Medium for a Tarot reading and she was the one who spoke to Aleister and asked him to contact me. The Medium said after all the disappointments in my life I could do with some success and she said these people could bring me success." As Peter said this, he suddenly realised what smell it was that pervaded the air in this house, it wasn't violets as he thought, it was the sweet smell of success! He had no idea how he knew that. He looked around him and saw that all the guests looked well dressed, even wealthy and they all talked with assurance and confidence. "Is Carrie your real name? Aleister said everyone is allocated a new name." "Yes it is my real name, but that's because I am not a proper member yet." As Peter talked to Carrie he found out she was also new to the group. She was only allowed at certain meetings. Carrie said she had to be sworn to secrecy, dedicated and initiated and her new name would be given to her then. Peter realised as they chatted Carrie was also attracted by the wealth and success.

"I am not allowed to tell you much, as you are not part of this group yet." Carrie said. "Aleister will explain more if you are invited back. I can tell you that in December the members look forward to the Winter Solstice on the 21st to 22nd December. There are Yuletide celebrations between 23rd and 25th December. But I am very lucky because if I am invited to be initiated that could happen as soon as 2nd February, at the celebration called Candlemass. However Aleister said it may happen even earlier as he is planning a special honour for me for Candlemass.

** The Sigil of Baphomet

Aleister said they will prepare me closer to the time. I can't wait though, I need some excitement and success in my life. Aleister tells me I will get power over my life and power to influence others so I will get what I want in the future." As she said this Peter could see Carrie's beautiful eyes sparkle with anticipation. At that moment Aleister returned and said that Peter needs to leave now. Peter hadn't even had a drink yet and hadn't met any of the other guests but he let Aleister lead him back to the front door.

Back in the entrance hall the same servant appeared holding Peter's coat and passed it to him. "I'll contact you soon Peter, don't worry" Aleister said, as the big oak double doors slid silently open as if by magic. As Aleister shook Peter's hand, Peter felt Aleister's hand seemed cold but also seemed to be very strong for a man of his age. Aleister smiled at him, but Peter felt a cold shiver run through his body, Aleister seemed to look through Peter, into his very soul. Peter was now in the doorway and as Aleister turned and walked back inside, the great entrance doors started to close. Peter again felt a cold shiver but this time it was the cold night air. It had already got dark, but as Peter walked down the steps the floodlights came on, there were obviously motion detectors. He turned up his collar as he continued down the steps towards his car. Looking at all the parked cars he suddenly realised that the little white Suzuki was probably Carrie's car. All the other cars were really expensive and Carrie like himself, was new and itching for some of this wealth and success. On an impulse Peter took out his mobile phone and photographed the Suzuki including the registration number. Peter climbed into his little car and drove slowly back to Brighton.

He had been on "auto pilot" all the way home and couldn't really remember the journey when he did get home. Peter lived in a small flat he rented in Brighton. Going up Middle Street, just before the ninety degree bend to the right and the pub called The Victory, there's a turning on the left called Benson Lane. Peter's flat was about ten yards up on the right above one of the many boutiques in that area. The area was cramped and noisy but with a pub close by and every type of eating place and takeaway you could think of in walking distance, the flat was very convenient. That is, excepting parking. When he first took the flat he had horrendous problems finding somewhere to park but now he had at last got a residents parking permit. He could now always find a parking place but it was often hundreds of yards from his flat which wasn't much fun when he had all the food shopping in the car or it was raining heavily, or both.

When he got indoors his little black cat he had recently got from a rescue centre came towards him and started to circle and meow, Sooty (not exactly an original name) was hungry, so he fed her. His head was full of the sights and sounds at the Pinnacle but mainly of thoughts of Carrie. He couldn't remember when he had met a more beautiful woman and it had been a while since he had been in the company of any young lady. His relationship had broken up nearly six months ago and he had been feeling too sorry for himself to date anyone. He then lost his job in an estate agent, because he had become depressed and had lost his focus. Everyone runs down estate agencies but he had enjoyed working there and because of his job he had found his own little flat which he loved. He then had no girlfriend or job and of course no money which put his flat at risk. He had also ignored his friends, even the ones that tried to help him. Now, at least, he had found a job, waiting on tables in a seafront café. It was hard work, long hours and poor pay but it paid the rent, was a lively café and that's where he met Josephine, the Medium.

Josephine had sat down in the café and asked him for a coffee. They got talking and she seemed to know he needed help and guidance. She persuaded him to come to her flat for a reading (Tarot Cards) and something made him jump at it but strangely it wasn't because he wanted to be alone with her. Also strange was the fact that, as Josephine was leaving the café, she turned back and asked him if he was a Christian and had he been baptised. He said no to both questions. The next night at the reading Jo told him about his mother and how he missed her. How he was suffering, especially since the girlfriend had gone, how he had lost his job and how his new job was dead end with no future. She said she'll ask someone called Aleister to ring him who will turn his life around.

Now, he had met a beautiful lady and a group of people that may be able to help him improve his lot. He had worries though. Peter was not well read and knew nothing of the occult, let alone Satanism but he wasn't stupid either and the sight of the goats head (Goat of Mendes) and Carrie talking of initiation gave Peter serious concerns. One of Peter's friends, he had unfortunately ignored recently, was a Pagan high priest and he promised himself he would talk to Steve about what he had seen today. But first he would make a few enquiries. Peter wasn't really into technology but he did have a laptop and knew how to search on the web. Peter 'googled' Satanism and initiation and what he found did not help to put his mind at rest. By now it was nearly midnight so Peter showered and prepared for bed. Peter noticed he was "sensitised", sort of jumpy. He kept looking behind himself, even though he knew the house was secure and he was alone. The last time he felt like this was when he was about 12 years of age and watched a scary movie he shouldn't have. He tried to ignore it, poured a double scotch and climbed into bed. However he fell asleep quickly but was dreaming and in the dreams kept seeing one minute Carrie's beautiful eyes and the next Aleister's eyes, not so comforting.

Peter woke feeling well rested and fresh but still couldn't concentrate on anything, his head full of The House, Carrie and Aleister. He was relieved he had the day off. He must go and see Steve as soon as possible. Steve might be home that day as Steve spent most of his time on Pagan matters. He was a self employed taxi driver and didn't work more than two days a week. After Peter had washed and breakfasted he telephoned Steve and was surprised how relieved he was when Steve said he was home for the day. Steve agreed to let him come round right away. It left Steve wondering what was wrong. He hadn't seen Peter for months and now Peter had to see him immediately. Peter drove round to Steve's house. Very different from The Pinnacle. Steve Connors lived in a small three bedroomed semi in Polegate, just north of Eastbourne. Peter met Steve by selling him his little house when Peter was still at the estate agency. Peter knew that being the top man in the local Pagan coven didn't bring many financial benefits and Steve had only been able to buy the house due to a small inheritance from his mother. Steve at 54 years of age was more than twenty years older than Peter but they enjoyed each-others company and had become friends. Steve opened his front door, he looked well. He welcomed Peter inside and asked if he wanted coffee. "Yes please", Peter said, "milk, no sugar, in case you can't remember". "Yes, it's been a while, hasn't it?" Steve replied. As Peter walked down the hall he saw on the wall above the kitchen door a Pentagram. It was similar to the one at The Pinnacle but the other way up. There was one point at the top, not two. Peter had seen this Pentagram at Steve's house a few times and knew this sign wasn't ominous.

When the coffee was made they went into Steve's lounge and made themselves comfortable. "What's the crisis Peter?" Steve said. "I don't hear from you for months and then suddenly you have to see me urgently!" Peter told Steve what had been happening to him starting back at the breakup of his relationship. "After Sue and I broke up and I moved out, I was at an all time low. I couldn't concentrate at work and ended up making mistakes and got fired. The only good thing was that I had found a nice little flat over at Brighton through the agency. I went to the Salvation Army shop and chose all the furniture and everything I needed in one go and they delivered it. I still found the flat empty and cold though, so I went to the rescue centre and got a little cat but it didn't help much. When I lost my job I couldn't pay the rent but I managed to get a job in a café on the front in Brighton. I have now paid the outstanding rent arrears, so that's ok." "I am very sorry you have had all this trouble and saddened you didn't come to me earlier but I feel this is not why you need to see me" Steve said. "No, not exactly" Peter replied. Peter then explained what had happened over the last two weeks. "So I went and saw this Medium, Josephine, for a Tarot reading and she persuaded me to go and see some people in Bridlington. She thought they will help me regain some control in my life". "So, who are these people Peter?"

As Peter told where he went and who he met Steve sat further forward in his chair and Peter could see he was taking in everything he said, every detail. At the end of Peter's story Steve simply said "and what is it you want from me?" "If you know, I would like to know who I am dealing with and what are the dangers if any". Steve replied "I know we haven't seen each-other for some time but we have been good friends in the past so I want to really tell you as much as I can, but that will take time. Have you got time?" "Absolutely Steve, I would appreciate it very much". "OK then, I'll make some more coffee, you'll need it".

After Steve made the coffee they returned to the lounge and Steve started to explain what Peter was getting into. "You have visited the home of a high priest of a Satanic Coven. They will all call themselves different names, usually from past Satanic disciples. Aleister no doubt takes his name from Aleister Crowley. He lived between 1875 and 1947. He lived the last part of his life just up the road in Hastings and was considered by some to have been one of the greatest British occultists. I don't know this group you have visited at all but Satanic covens are usually very secretive. Satanic covens can be of many different types. Some are fairly benign, that is harmless but some are very very dangerous. Do you intend to see them again if invited?" "Yes" Peter said, "If only to see Carrie again. But I do need to understand who and what they are, and if I join them whether I can change my mind later".

"That's difficult Peter. There are many types of Satanic groups but you could divide the groups or covens into two categories. Atheistic Satanists and Theistic Satanists. The first type Atheistic Satanists see Satan as a symbol of human desires. They practice what Aleister Crowley called "Do what thou wilt" which basically means there are no rules and the members do anything they like, morally that is. They see mankind as animals in an amoral universe. The Coven often have a lot of sexual rituals and practice sorcery (magick) to increase their influence over other people. In these types of covens usually the members can join in or not as they want and members aren't forced. Their magick comes from their own minds and influence.

** A Typical Pagan Pentagram

The second type or Theistic Satanists can be very different. They worship Satan as a supernatural deity, a God. In these covens there are very strict rules. Members have to dedicate themselves to Satan and then be initiated into the coven. They sign in their own blood, literally. They are locked in for life because as part of their initiation they have to renounce the Christian God and Jesus. This precludes them from rescue by the forces of the light. They are not allowed to leave. Some of the rituals are mandatory and sexual rituals may be enforced. Peter, these people are serious shit!"

"Why would anyone want to join this type of coven?" Peter said. "Because Peter it's the real thing. Atheistic Satanism is for people who want an excuse to do anything they like. To feed their desires. To behave badly. But they have limited powers. I say limited not powerless, so don't be misled. But Theistic Satanism is worshipping the Devil himself. His disciples can achieve great powers and be very dangerous people to deal with. They believe in and do communicate with demons and the Devil himself and can even invoke them. They can bring these creatures into this world. With Theistic Satanists if you clash with them you may not just be fighting evil people but the Devil himself. I have spent forty years studying paganism and magick and understand how to protect myself but if this Aleister is the High Priest of a Theistic Coven and if he is a Magus or heaven forbid an Ipsissimus, he is to be seriously feared by all. Me included. If you go back and find they are a Theistic Coven leave immediately and never return for any reason".

"But I still don't understand Steve, how could this Aleister, even if he does lead a Theistic Coven, force me to do anything, such as stop me leaving the coven even if I have signed in blood." "Forgetting Satan himself for a second, as I said Aleister will be a Magus or Ipsissimus, and will have powers himself to control you" said Steve. "What powers could Aleister have?" "As a Magus he will have several powers which he can use to control anyone. For example he will have been given the gift of hypnotism which he'll use to persuade people to do what he wants. More seriously than that he will be gifted in delivering the evil eye. The eyes are the only part of the body that is not protected by flesh and bone and is the direct route to the brain. He will be able just by glancing into your eyes to implant thoughts, fears and desires not of your own. If this man turns out to be the Master of a Theistic Coven do not look him in the eyes. He will also be able to scry." "What's scry?" Peter asks. "He was probably brought up from childhood learning to scry. Scrying means to perceive or to reveal. You can use a crystal ball, a candle flame or mirror but he will use water.

As a Satanic High Priest he will have a Christian Baptismal Font stolen from a church. This will be in his house and will have been desecrated by Satanic spells and he will have it full with water which he will have blessed as "holy water". A large black candle will continuously burn next to the font. He will use the font like you would use CCTV except that he has no boundaries, none at all. If he looks for you he will find you and see you wherever you are and whatever you are doing. If he finds you asleep and he has already given you the evil eye you are at great risk. If Aleister is an Ipsissimus he can invoke the demons and force them to his will. His power is without equal. My advice is not to go back there under any circumstances."

***The Baphomet or Goat of Mendes

"Steve, so if it's so dangerous and scary I still don't understand why anyone would join these covens?" Steve replied "You tell me Peter, I've told you how dangerous it is and you are still thinking about going back. People are attracted by the power and influence they may get over others, some are attracted by possible wealth whilst some just join for the sex. You must ask yourself what it is that attracts you and is it really worth those risks. You can lose your soul Peter."

Peter said "You were talking earlier about sex rituals. I think I understand why the Atheistic Satanists perform them, for pure pleasure but why do Theistic Satanists perform sexual rituals, is that also only for pure pleasure?" Steve replied "The old religions are based on the earth, sun and moon, the stars, the seasons, farming and the cycle of life. Basically that is fertility, birth and death. Sexual orgasm is creating life and therefore apart from killing it is the most powerful thing we can do with our bodies. Harness human sacrifice or sexual orgasm to a ritual or spell and it increases its effectiveness tenfold. Sexual rituals are safer and more pleasurable than human sacrifice. Early pagan farmers would make love with their wives in the middle of the field in spring in worship of the Goddess Eostra to enhance the field's fertility. This was not perverted, it was their belief and custom. The Satanists have taken the principle from the pagans and extended it to sexual perversions. You still worship Eostra today Peter." "How do you work that out Steve, I have never even heard the name." "Aah Peter but you have. Every spring we give each-other eggs and celebrate Easter. Eostra is the pagan Goddess of fertility and every spring we give each-other eggs in rememberance of her, asking her to make our fields and cattle fertile. We eat rabbit or hare as they are her familiars, ever heard of Easter bunnies? The Romans changed the name from Eostra to Easter and forced the people to remember Jesus not the Goddess. It only half worked as we still like eggs and bunnies and deep down we believe in the need for fertility in Spring."

"Wow Steve, I never knew that although I must admit I did always wonder what chocolate eggs and bunnies had to do with Jesus's death and resurrection. Steve, can I ask one last thing and I'll leave you to have a peaceful Saturday. If I do go back to the house how would I know what type of Satanists they are?"

"You would be putting yourself at great risk, but if you were able to look around the house there will be a room where they perform rituals. On the wall will be a representation of Satan, the Goat of Mendes. It will have the body of a human female, the head and feet of a goat, the wings of an angel and a pentacle on its forehead. The room will have a large square drawn on the floor with another large square within it.

Between these lines will be the names of the four angels and inside this will be about four circles. There will be strange writings and symbols but what you are looking for is a separate unattached circle with a triangle inside it. That is where they invoke the demons. If you see that, your body and your very soul are at risk if you stay with this group. In fact you need to immediately run out that building and never ever return. In those circumstances I would actually advise you to find a Roman Catholic church and ask the Priest to hear your confession and give you absolution."

"I will sleep on what you have told me Steve. Thank you very much. Can I come back and talk again sometime?" "If you have returned to this group and I sense you have received the evil eye or have a familiar, a demon with you, then no. I will see you but somewhere else. You will not be welcome to enter my home." "Thank you for your time and advice Steve. I will think on everything you have told me." Peter stood up and made his way to the front door. When they shook hands Steve took his hand in both of his, squeezed tightly and looked deeply into Peter's eyes and Peter felt Steve was looking for something in his eyes. Peter drove home to Brighton. More knowledgeable but more worried.

Peter relaxed on Sunday. Watched a bit of football and had a few beers he had in the fridge. The cat seemed very affectionate, climbed on his lap every time he sat down. Could she feel the tension in Peter or was she coming into season? Peter was working all week but had Saturday off again, which was unusual and lovely. Saturday morning he had a lie in and was woken by the phone ringing. He rolled over and grabbed the receiver and froze when he heard the rich deep voice of Aleister. During the week Peter had decided not to go back to The Pinnacle but when Aleister invited him to visit him tonight he found himself saying yes and asking how he should dress and whether he should bring anything. "Dress casually Peter in whatever makes you feel comfortable. There will only be three of us. Very informal. As there's not a celebration or meeting of the group tonight I am taking the opportunity to make a personal invitation to you and Carrie, to give us a chance to talk and get to know each-other without other people distracting us. A chance for me to tell you about our group and for you to ask questions. If you want what we can give you, it's important you know what we want from you. Use a taxi so you can relax and drink. I'll expect you at nine this evening." As Peter put down the phone he felt his heart hammering in his chest. He felt scared and elated at once. Still he had agreed, he couldn't not go, and at any rate a chance to see Carrie again.

*** 'The Fallen Angel'. Satan in "Paradise Lost," as illustrated by Gustave Dore.

CHAPTER 2

The Temple

Peter couldn't think of anything else all day other than the meeting that night. He really wasn't sure about his emotions at all. He was one minute thinking of Carrie and fantasizing about her, well it had been a long time since he slept with a woman and the next minute in panic and turmoil about meeting Aleister again. Funny thing is, he was sure Aleister knew he would come, in which case Aleister knew he wasn't working and didn't have other arrangements. These thoughts immediately brought back what Steve was saying last Saturday, that Aleister could possibly be able to see him by scrying and might already have the evil eye on him. But immediately he started thinking like that he dismissed it. Steve is just scaring him to stop him going back to that group and he had only spent a couple of minutes with Aleister last week. Nothing happened then, he was sure.

He would have to leave his flat tonight at seven thirty to be sure to be on time. That A27 from Brighton to Eastbourne is an unpredictable road at the best of times and Saturday evenings it could be especially bad. He would have another shower and shave at six, especially for Carrie's benefit and then have a light snack and relax before his drive. Aleister had said take a taxi but Peter couldn't afford a taxi from Brighton to Bridlington and he didn't intend to drink much at any rate. He wanted to keep a clear head. The day dragged, the hours crept by. He felt like a child on Christmas eve. After his shower and shave Peter decided to wear a new pair of jeans he hadn't worn yet and an open neck shirt.

And then it was seven thirty in the evening and Peter was ready to go. As he drove he started thinking about Carrie again and made a mental note to get her full name and a telephone number. First excuse he gets, he must ask her for her number. It would be really good if he could meet Carrie privately, another night, just the two of them. He would love to compare notes with her. Hear what she is thinking, hear what are her needs and her goals. Is she scared? Does she worry about Aleister and his possible powers? And then he thought about Aleister, he must avoid eye contact if possible, without being rude. It would also be good if he can persuade Aleister to give them the grand tour of his lovely house. Maybe Aleister will show them where they celebrate in the house, assuming they do celebrate there of course. He arrived at the large metal latticed green gates. He was early, only twenty to nine. Peter was about to get out the car when the gates started to open. Yes, of course, the eyes of the Griffins. The staff had probably noted his car and registration number already. He drove up the long driveway and this time there was only one car parked there, a little white Suzuki. He had been right. That was Carrie's car and she was even earlier than him.

He parked and as he got out the cold reminded him it was getting closer to Christmas. He walked up the entrance steps and the great entrance doors started to open before he even reached the top step. This time the servant was waiting for him and he held out his hand for Peter's coat. After taking his coat the servant just turned and walked through the double doors into the lounge without saying a word. Peter assumed he was to follow. In the lounge sat Aleister and Carrie. They both stood up as Peter walked in. Aleister was wearing what was once called a smoking jacket. A purple jacket with black silk collar and cuffs, but Peter only had eyes for Carrie. She too was casual, in jeans and blouse but the jeans were tight and accentuated her long shapely legs whilst the blouse showed enough cleavage to be sexy without being inappropriate. Her long blond hair and blue eyes completed the effect. She was stunning. They all warmly greeted each-other and Aleister waved Peter to a comfortable chair next to where the other two had been seated.

"I welcome you both again to my home" Aleister said "and would like to offer you both a glass of white wine, a very pleasant Chablis." As he said this his servant reappeared with a silver tray and three glasses of wine. They each took a glass and Aleister continued. "Before I go any further I have to stress in the strongest terms that everything you hear and see this evening is kept in strictest confidence. You must remain totally silent to all outsiders, only talking to other members of the group about what you hear and see in these walls. Is that understood?" Carrie and Peter both agreed. "If you cannot remain silent outside these walls to non members you must leave now". Again Carrie and Peter both said yes.

"We are a secret society, a satanic coven" Aleister continued "nothing that happens here is illegal but we jealously guard our privacy. The name of Satan comes from the original Sanskrit and means "truth". You will learn much over the next few months. This will be a very exciting time for you both. An adventure into things spiritual and magickal you could not have even dreamed of. Are you both sure you wish to continue?" Again they both nodded and said yes.

Aleister moved his chair closer to Carrie and lent forward in his chair. He then held out his hands and told Carrie to hold his hands. Carrie put down her glass of wine and held Aleister's hands. He told Carrie to stare, to focus on his middle eye, between his eyes and just above his eyes, basically between his eyebrows. He did the same and said "Do you swear you will not tell anyone outside our group what you will hear and see inside these walls at anytime, now or in the future? Say I do." Aleister appeared to tighten his grip slightly and Carrie seemed to shake slightly as she said I do. As Aleister let go of Carrie's hands Carrie looked as though she was in a trance. Aleister then moved his chair to face Peter and repeated this procedure. When Aleister looked into Peter's eyes Peter felt totally vulnerable, he felt as though Aleister was looking at his entire life and every secret he had and through to his very soul. Peter also shook when Aleister gripped his hands as Peter said I do. The process was not unpleasant but it was the most scary thing that Peter had ever done or had done to him. He now felt like he imagined he would feel, after surviving a bungee jump.

"You both are now members of our group. However you have a long way to go before you are truly one of us and I'll explain that now. Our secret society is a group of members most of whom you briefly saw last week, and which you both now belong. Within that group is a privileged number that are permitted to join the coven when we work in the circle, celebrate or worship. You have to earn that right, that status, to join our coven. When the coven forms there is a maximum of thirteen including myself as High Priest. The maximum number in the coven is thirteen because there are thirteen full moons in a lunar year and thirteen chakras of the soul. As you may know Jesus chose twelve disciples so that their gathering, including himself, was thirteen, for the very same reasons. The coven is a powerful group, the more powerful the minds of the members, the more powerful the coven. The coven creates energy and power by regular meetings and rituals. By doing certain exercises and performing certain rituals the coven develops a powerful aura of energy, a cone of power and from this comes a bonding of the souls and the coven works as one. Some of these rituals enlist the help of demons who will assist us in our endeavours and who will also increase the power of the coven. If any member is in need the coven comes together to help. The coven becomes closely knit and becomes your family."

"There is a hierarchy in the coven. Each member must take a vow of secrecy, which you have now done. Then we prepare you for a dedication ritual to Satan. This is followed by preparation for the initiation rite. After initiation you will be given a new name in Satan which from then onwards will be the only name you will be known by in our group. You will learn the name of the patron Demoness and the Sigil of that Patron Demoness will be sewn upon your robe. We like to celebrate 'sky clad' but frequently have to celebrate in our robes, for practical purposes, especially for ceremonies outdoors in the winter. We will give you a copy of the satanic calendar which shows the Esbats (full moons), the Sabbats (Holy Days) and Greater Sabbats, these dates align with important astral energies and therefore attendance is required, no exceptions. You will be granted spiritual gifts and develop personal powers as you progress, which you can use to gain influence over others outside of our group. But all will be revealed in time." He turned and looked at Carrie, deeply into her eyes. "I must tell you Carrie that I have already chosen you for a special task, a great responsibility but also a great honour. You will be a guide, a type of minder, carer, for a young girl who will be joining us in the next few weeks. You will help prepare her for her role which will be a great honour for her."

With that Aleister rose and said "I have said enough for now and will show you our beautiful Temple as promised." Peter and Carrie naturally stood and followed Aleister out into the entrance hall. Aleister led them up the nearest, right side, staircase to the balcony above. In the centre of the balcony was a door which Aleister went through. Peter followed him through the door and found a long corridor with several doors leading off it on both sides. This is a very large house, Peter thought. At the end of the corridor it opened out into a circular vestibule with comfy chairs around the walls. It could be a doctor's waiting room, without the magazines, except the carpet and furniture looked and probably were very expensive. Deep pile light brown carpet, immaculately painted cream walls and woodwork, and leather and mahogany chairs. But Peter hardly noticed any of this, his eyes were fixed on the double doors in the centre of the facing wall. The two doors were made with a lovely curve at the top, fitting into the surrounding archway. They were the same type as the main entrance doors and nearly as large but these doors were gold. Not painted gold but Peter assumed they were gold leaf on the entire surface of both doors and the archway. Each door had a round and ornate door knob that was also gold. The centre area of both doors was flat and in the middle they both had the same sign, a symbol, in what looked like black mosaic. The effect was literally breath taking. Peter had no idea what the signs were but every fibre of his body and soul told him it was significant and malevolent. The signs were The Sigil of Lucifer (Satan).

**The Sigil of Lucifer (Satan)

A Sigil is a symbol that signifies a fallen angel or demon and it helps to create a bond between the demon and sorcerer who attempts to use the demon to carry out his own desires. Invoking demons is physically and spiritually dangerous, but this Sigil represents the Devil himself. Even contemplating invoking the Devil severely frightens the bravest of men and women. The fact that these doors had the Devil's Sigil on them was very worrying and frightening. It indicated to anyone educated in the Black Arts that this Temple had in fact been used to invoke the Devil himself. Peter did not understand any of this but something inside of him warned him of major danger.

Aleister lent forward and taking hold of the two door knobs, pulled open the doors. As Peter saw the interior of the Temple his head spun, his knees went weak and he struggled to breath. The Temple was huge and very ornate but what struck Peter was the floor. The floor was white. It had hand made Italian white tiles laid throughout the entire Temple floor. On these tiles were markings made in what looked like black mosaic. The drawings and writings and symbols were exactly as Steve had described to Peter last week. It was absolutely spectacular but the severe warnings that Steve had given Peter was about these very markings. Steve had said that if he sees these markings he must run away in fear for his life and even his soul.

Peter was definitely in shock. He had heard everything Steve had warned him about but he didn't really expect to be presented with it. As Peter struggled with dizziness and his breathing he suddenly became aware that Aleister was closely watching him. After opening the doors and walking into the Temple, Aleister had turned around and had immediately seen that Peter seemed to be in distress. Peter realising he was under close scrutiny forced himself to breath slowly and deeply, then smiling he turned and looked at Aleister and said "Wow, the Temple is magnificent, it literally took my breath away. I had no idea it would be like this. I just expected a room where you celebrate, not this gold temple of wonder.

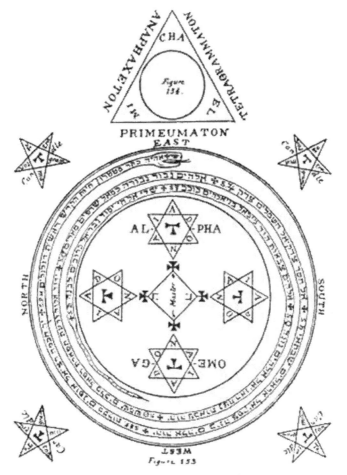

***This magick circle is attributed to King Solomon.
It is similar to that drawn on the floor of The Temple
at The Pinnacle. This circle is especially designed for
evocation, when a demon is commanded to appear.
The conjuror works in the large circle and the demon is
summoned to the separate triangle in the East,
so the conjuror is protected.

Aleister seemed to relax and replied "I take that as a compliment
Peter and I am pleased to see you like it so much. The Temple is for
Satan and for his worship, so it is essential it is grand and beautiful.
Always remember he is the truth. Now," Aleister continued "I regret
I have to bring our meeting to a close." As he said this Aleister

started to walk out the Temple and once Carrie and Peter were out he carefully closed the great golden doors. They followed him down the same staircase they went up and to the entrance doors which were now opening towards them. When Aleister shook Peter's hand he felt Aleister look deep into his eyes and felt there was no secret he would be able to keep from him. For some reason only now did he suddenly remember Steve's warning of the evil eye, and realised it was probably too late. They both said goodbye to Aleister, who promised he would contact them soon.

It was dark and as before the parking area lights came on automatically. As Carrie and Peter walked towards their cars, Peter said "I need to talk to you Carrie. I don't want you to think this is some sort of pick up. I need to talk to you and tonight. I will not sleep tonight. I have too many scary thoughts in my head. Aleister said we cannot talk to anyone outside the membership and I have the feeling he will know if we do. For me, that leaves you. You are the only other member I know and can therefore talk to. Please can I follow you home and talk to you over coffee?" Carrie thought for a short while then said "Yes that will be fine. I also feel we have seen a great deal tonight, and I will sleep better if I get to talk it through and get my feelings out as well. I live in Wychamton, the other side of Seaford. You said you live in Brighton so you can easily go on from there. You can follow me." "Can I take your mobile telephone number?" Peter replied, "Just in case I lose you on route. I don't know that area well." Peter punched Carrie's number into his phone and then climbed into his car and started up. He followed Carrie's white Suzuki down the driveway and noticed in the mirror the lights go off behind him. As they approached, the big green gates slowly swung open.

Carrie took the country lane back to Stone Cross, turning right at the traffic lights, towards the A22. When she hit the roundabout of the A22 she turned south to Eastbourne. Carrie led Peter through Eastbourne and onto the A259 to Seaford. The other side of Seaford she turned right to Wychamton and as they drove through the village she stopped outside a small pretty country cottage. It was now very dark but the street lamps were still on and bright enough to see the cottage and its entrance quite clearly. Carrie fumbled for her key and let them both in. "Is tea or coffee ok?" she said, walking down the narrow hall to the kitchen at the back. "Tea's fine" said Peter "I'm going to have trouble sleeping any-rate, so I'll avoid the coffee thanks."

They sat down and made themselves comfortable in Carrie's small lounge. "I have to tell you something Carrie," Peter said "I was very worried after my visit to Aleister's house the previous Friday evening, so the next day I went and saw a friend of mine who is a pagan high priest". Peter then went on to tell Carrie everything that Steve had said, finishing with his warning about the ceremonial markings especially the triangle in a separate circle used for invoking demons. Carrie listened carefully to everything Peter said and remained completely calm. "Peter, as far as I am concerned its like this. I'll be frank with you. Many ladies would be very happy if they had my looks and I am also blessed that my parents have left me a lovely cottage which is all paid for, but unfortunately it is not enough for me. I don't know why but I have a very strong need to have wealth and power. Even with everything I have, or maybe because of what I have, on several occasions people have taken advantage of me and abused me."

"Am I allowed to ask, Carrie, in what way were you abused? Financially or physically?" "No, not like you are thinking Peter. I am talking emotionally. People have made promises they didn't keep, made me offers that didn't happen, stuff like that. Each time I wanted to strike back but couldn't. Wanted to hurt someone but didn't know how. I actually got to a point of thinking of suicide. I know its crazy but that's how I felt. Then I was introduced to Aleister and talking to him and his members it became obvious to me that if I went down their so called left hand path, as long as I did everything asked of me, I would gain power to influence others. With that power I can become wealthy and can hurt people who mistreat me." "But Carrie," Peter replied "you will have to debase yourself and you will be putting yourself at enormous risk." "Peter, I don't care about all that. Everyone of those members you saw that Friday night has debased themselves, as you call it. Everyone of them has put themselves at risk, but they followed the Path and did what was asked of them and are now being rewarded. I don't want to go through life without power to influence and hurt when I want to. They are fine, why shouldn't I be?"

"Carrie, I am truly shocked. I really didn't expect any of that from you. However I can relate to what you are saying. My Mother passed away suddenly, no warning, shortly afterwards my girlfriend throws me out and then I get sacked at work. I nearly became a beach bum! Luckily I got a new job and have kept my flat. Still, it doesn't seem fair. I also feel like I want to hurt someone but I don't know who. Power and wealth are very attractive to me as well." "Then my dear Peter we need to join the group and carefully follow the Path." "What is this Path Carrie?" "Aleister explained to me that there are two Paths, the right hand Path to the Christian God and the Left hand Path to Satan, the Truth. Everyone has heard Satan looks after his own, so you just need to learn and obey, and we'll be fine."

Peter replied "Steve said that we can change direction, change our minds up to the point of dedication. When we dedicate ourselves to Satan we also renounce all other Gods including the Christian God and of course Jesus. Steve said that once we have renounced Jesus we cannot call upon the forces of the light to help us, to save us. We cannot change direction. We are committed to Satan." "But, Peter, you said Steve is a pagan and therefore doesn't believe Jesus is the son of God, so how can he say that." "Carrie, Steve doesn't but we do believe that, that's the point. Because we believe that, we are turning from the light, from the forces of good, whatever they maybe, Pagan, Christian, Jewish, Buddhism." "OK, Peter, I get the point, we abide by the rules and go along with everything but when it gets to dedication we need to be one hundred per cent sure. Is that about right?" "Yes, that is about right Carrie. Can I ask one thing though, I noticed all the members were standing in pairs. I get the feeling that's what happens when they have meetings, worship and celebrations. I can cope with all this, if we can do it together. Are you OK with that?" Again Carrie thought for a short while, then said "That's fine Peter, it doesn't matter to me who my partner is, I am doing this for all the reasons I explained. It can just as easily be with you as anyone else. Just stick to the rules. Do not tell anyone outside anything, especially not Steve. If you must talk, talk to me, OK? If you put me at risk I'll sacrifice you first. Do you understand me?" "Yes Carrie, I understand, I will stick to all the rules and not talk to anyone but you." "Then, Peter, we will be fine".

They both realised it was getting very late, and everything that needed to be said, had been said. Peter finished his tea and shook Carrie's hand and left. He drove back onto the A259 and carried onto Newhaven. At Newhaven he turned right and drove north until he joined the A27 to Brighton. Amazingly Peter slept really well. He had expected to toss and turn but he slept the sleep of the contented. Even the thoughts and images of Carrie didn't disturb him.

CHAPTER 3

The Gift

Peter woke feeling fine. It was Sunday and a day of rest. He had to work six days in a row from tomorrow so he'd make a point of relaxing today. He washed, shaved and dressed and went round the corner to a little café that he knew was open on Sundays and did a good breakfast. He had a full English breakfast excepting the beans, couldn't handle them this early. Then he went for a stroll around the area, always interesting, especially on Sunday mornings. There were always NFAs (no fixed abodes) in corners and shop doorways. Also drunks that had passed out and never made it home and of course druggies that had nearly killed themselves by trying something new or that little bit more. Brighton seems to attract the flotsam of life, and Peter knew it was really easy to become one. On the other hand there were always people giving out tracts trying to sell salvation in the name of Jesus or playing tambourines singing Hade Krishna. Plus joggers in track suits trying to lose weight, get fitter or honing their bodies to perfection. It seemed like the full spectrum of humanity was represented on the streets of Brighton on Sundays mornings. It should depress him, but the truth (he'll never openly admit) was that he had come close to joining the drop outs, the NFAs and it made him feel good that he had avoided it. He made his way back to his flat and after a few domestic chores he planned to spend the rest of the day in an armchair watching TV or reading. That changed when Carrie rang him later in the day.

During the morning, Aleister telephoned Carrie. Somehow she knew it was him as she picked up the phone. Not guessed but actually knew for certain it was him. Aleister explained to Carrie that he knew she was in a hurry to commit and progress. He said he was less sure of Peter who is always looking for the exit door. Carrie said "Not to worry Aleister, Peter will come along with me. He will do whatever I say. My hold over him is the oldest hold a woman can have over a man. Don't worry Aleister, Peter is totally with us." "As I said Carrie, I have a special responsibility, a special honour for you but the time frame is tight. I want you to prepare Gwendoline for her honour at the Candlemass celebration which is on 2nd February. That means you have to be dedicated and initiated before then. We have one of our most important nights of the year, the Winter Solstice on 21st December but that is only 7 nights away and I want you and Peter to make your dedications on that night. That then gives us a month to prepare you both for initiation on 7th January, St. Winebald's Day and we can then prepare Gwendoline for the Candlemass celebration on 2nd February." "What do you want us both to do then Aleister?" "I want you Carrie, to take the lead. You alone come to my house at 9pm tonight and collect the papers for dedication. I will go through them with you. You and Peter must then go through these papers so you are fully prepared for the Winter Solstice." Carrie replied "I'll see you tonight at 9." "Yes, I won't keep you too long Carrie."

Carrie had been preparing her late breakfast when Aleister had rung. She decided to enjoy her 'brunch' and rang Peter later and asked him what time he finished work tomorrow. "Normally home by 8 o'clock" he said. "Great, can you be at my cottage by 9pm?" "What's the occasion Carrie?" "I collect our dedication papers tonight from Aleister and we only have 6 days to go through them. I'll see you then" she said and hung up.

Suddenly Peter's quiet Sunday had changed. He was panicking. He immediately rang Steve and told him about the dedication papers. Steve went ballistic. "You not only ignored my warnings not to go back there but you are now preparing to dedicate your life and soul to Satan, are you completely mad?" "I, sort of, am being carried along Steve" "By who?" Steve replied. "Her name's Carrie, Steve, and I think I am infatuated." "Peter, can you hear yourself? You are being infatuated and carried along by Carrie. You aren't getting warning bells, Peter? Peter, I told you what you are dealing with. The High Priest is probably watching you right now. You cannot come round to my house, do you understand? You must not answer your phone, you must not go round to his house and you must not let anyone from their coven enter your flat. If you do want me to help you, I probably still can as you haven't been dedicated yet but you must do everything I say without any exceptions. I will need the help of my coven to protect you and maybe even the local Roman Catholic Priest. Trying to protect you will probably put us all at risk. You have no idea what you have done, Peter, but that is why we will try to help you. Are you going to do everything I say?" "I am not sure Steve. I think I do want to join them. I have nothing else going for me in my life. I am seriously attracted to their power and wealth, and of course Carrie." "So why did you ring me Peter?" "I don't really know, it's a bit like a suicide ringing to say they are going to do it. I can't stop but I want someone to know." "Peter, I can't help unless you are totally committed to wanting to get out and frankly I can't justify putting others at risk if you actually want to do this. I am going to hang up and talk to my coven members. You can't come round to my house, Peter, but you can telephone me and ask for help if you really mean it and are committed in leaving them, but only before you are dedicated. Do you understand?" "Yes Steve, thanks" and Peter hung up.

Later that day, 9 o'clock sharp, Carrie was climbing the front steps to the great entrance doors of Aleister's house. The doors started to silently swing inwards even before she made the top step. Aleister, in a brightly coloured waistcoat and silk cravat, was standing there waiting to greet her. He had a scroll of papers tied with black ribbon in his left hand. He smiled warmly, shook her hand and said welcome but she again noticed the coldness of his hand. He ushered her into his large lounge on the right of the entrance hall. He waved her towards a comfy seat and took the one opposite for himself. As they settled his servant arrived and nodded at Aleister. "Would you like a drink Carrie?" Aleister asked. "Only a lemonade if you have one thanks, I have to drive." Aleister ordered a scotch and water. As the servant left them, Aleister reached over to the side table and placed the scroll of papers on it.

"Let me explain the basic workings of a coven. I am talking about Theistic Covens, those that worship The Deity, Lucifer, Satan, the Truth, The Original Gods. Atheistic covens are a cult, an excuse to do what they like, without structure or reason, without a belief system. They don't actually believe in Satan, only in what they believe he stands for. We belong to a Theistic Coven which has an enforced set of rules and a strict hierarchy. The word coven comes from the latin conventus which means gathering or assembly. The words convene or convention have the same derivation. A coven should provide camaraderie, enjoyment of the practices and companionship. Membership of the coven should feel like belonging to a strong family. Members will help each-other in times of need. The purpose of the coven is to educate and train members, and encourage them to higher levels of worship, and power. The coven works to combine the growing individual powers of each member into a powerful aura of energy. To achieve this, the coven must meet very regularly to build this energy and to learn to work as a group and be able to effectively focus this energy in the interests of Satan. The individual members can also tap into this energy for their own desires and needs."

The servant returned and quietly placed their drinks beside them and as he left Aleister continued, "To achieve these goals, there must be rules which are enforced and members must be loyal, trustworthy, reliable and secretive but most of all as members of the coven we must be totally dedicated to Satan. It has always been known that Satan looks after his own. We become spiritually strong because Satan comes to us and gives us inner strength. He guides us and supports us. In return we have to commit ourselves to him and renounce all other Gods. Hence the dedication. In serving Satan we become a member of this powerful family and we also receive benefits. Some of these benefits will be by way of spiritual gifts given by Satan as rewards and some benefits will be earned as you move up the hierarchy and become more powerful as a member. As you know I am the High Priest. I am a Magus which gives me personal magickal powers. I am working towards Ipsissimus, the highest power for mortals. At your dedication you will meet the other coven members including the High Priestess, Dame Alice, she is also the executor of the coven and will deputise for me in my absence. Once you have been dedicated and initiated you and Peter will be mainly dealing with Dame Alice who manages the day to day issues of the members. You however, right now, just have to focus on dedication." "Can I ask you Aleister, what happens at dedication and what are the papers you mentioned?" asked Carrie.

"Dedication is simply making a commitment to Satan. As I said this means you have to renounce other Gods that you may have previously worshipped, for example the Christian God and Jesus. The ceremony is a simple one. The coven of 13 will be present, will form the circle and will have cleansed the circle and will have called the Patron Demoness Astaroth to witness on behalf of Satan. Astaroth may be present in spirit or if you are very blessed she may show herself. You and Peter will have bathed and be given robes to wear, called dominoes. The dominoes are clean and can only be put on when entering the circle. The principle is that you are making a prayer, a vow to Satan and nothing unclean from this world must enter the circle as a mark of respect to Astaroth and Satan. When you arrive at the circle you will be invited in by myself, at which point you slip on your domino and enter. You recite a prayer of commitment you have learnt with your hands together in prayer and your eyes upwards towards the sky or looking at Astaroth if she has shown herself. Then your finger will be pricked by Dame Alice and she will drain a little blood into a clean glass. You will be given a quill pen and you will sign in your blood on the altar the written copy of the prayer you have been holding. You then fold the prayer and burn it in the black candle before you, allowing the ashes to fall into the plate next to the candle. When the prayer is fully burnt to ash you cry out "So mote it be" and then follow with an even louder "Hail Satan". The ceremony is ended and you leave the circle." "Can I ask something Aleister?" "Of course, what is it you want to know?" "Can you explain who Astaroth is please."

Aleister replied "You may know her from your history lessons at school. She was worshipped and called Astarte by the Canaanites, then by the Sumerians as Inanna, she was called Ishtar by the Babylonians and the Assyrians worshipped her as Ashtoreth. The Egyptians called her Isis and in the Semitic language approximately 1500 BC she is named Anat. She was called Ashtaroth by the Phoenicians their Goddess of fertility, motherhood and war. Their Goddess of the Earth. She has been known for hundreds of years, sometimes referred to as a Goddess and sometimes referred to as a Demoness. You can call Astaroth many names but she is the power of fertility, motherhood and war. I should also mention that Astaroth is my personal Guardian Demoness as High Priest of the coven and a Magus. Anyone attacking me physically or spiritually may have to face her wroth. Astaroth was kind enough to consent to become the coven's Patron Demoness as well. You will see our dominoes have The Sigil of Astaroth embroided on them."

**The Sigil of Astaroth

"Thank you Aleister, but I am still a little confused. I am sure I have read that Pagans have always worshipped a Goddess of fertility. Is that the same Goddess?" Carrie asked. "You are right Carrie they do worship a Goddess of fertility, but that isn't Astaroth. The Goddess the Pagans worship is the Goddess the Greeks called Aphrodite and the Romans later called Venus. Celtic Pagans refer to her as Eostra the goddess of fertility and love, which is where the word Easter comes from. The Romans when they invaded Britain for the second time had by then become Christian and turned their back on the Pagan Gods. However they found that the Celts would not accept a single male God and still wanted a Goddess. So they called her the Mother of God, Mary of course. Even today many Roman Catholics pray to her not Jesus. Astaroth is the Goddess of fertility, motherhood and war, the Goddess of the Earth. She can be angry and aggressive which is why she is also known as a Demoness. I hope that is a little clearer for you.

You do not have to worry about this detail at this stage. After initiation you will have a mentor who will guide and teach you in all matters."

Aleister then said "We must return to the matter in hand, your Dedication. Once the ceremony is ended and you have left the circle you can keep the dominoes in place but only in the Temple. Return to the bathrooms and get changed. Your domino will be made for you personally and will have your name inside. Take the domino with you and leave. Thoroughly wash the domino when you get home. Do not ever wear it outside the circle unless you are leaving the circle and then change as soon as possible. To ignore this is to contaminate the domino which will contaminate you. Once you and Peter have left the Temple the coven members will start to celebrate your Dedications and The Winter Solstice, with eating and drinking and orgy. You cannot return to the Temple or stay at this time as you are not initiated members of the coven. You both must leave through another door, which we will show you and you should return home directly and spend the rest of the night alone in meditation and prayer to Satan. To answer your earlier question about the papers, I pass these to you now." Aleister lent across to Carrie and gave her the scroll of papers with the black ribbon. "These papers are a careful written description of the procedures of the dedication I have just described to you. Plus the prayer you must both now learn by heart. There are two copies of each, for yourself and Peter. You may bring both sets of papers with you on the night and you may refer to the procedures list before and during the dedication if you forget what to do but it is essential you have learnt the prayer by heart and can recite it with your eyes upward to Satan or looking at Astaroth if she is visually present. You Carrie, must now go through this with Peter and help him prepare. The regular practicing, learning the prayer by heart, is part of the initial dedication preparation. You assimilate the words and conviction into your very being. If you have any questions you are welcome to contact me. My telephone number is on the papers, which is confidential. Please do not forget that everything you have heard today and is written on those papers is extremely private and must remain within the members of the coven. I am aware of all indiscretions."

Aleister stood and as Carrie followed suit he said "Normally we celebrate Winter Solstice outside and sky-clad but because you and

Peter are making your dedications and you are not initiated yet we are making an exception and will be in the Temple. Ensure that you both arrive here on the evening of 21st December, no later than 10pm. Your ceremony starts at 11pm and must be concluded before midnight when the coven celebrate Winter Solstice." Carrie then asked Aleister what "sky-clad" meant. "Quite simply Carrie, it means you are solely clad by the sky, naked in other words. We don't refer to naked though, as we are all naked in many ways when we are before Satan." Aleister then explained that he mustn't detain her any longer and walked her to the front door. As he did so, Aleister said "During the next few days I will invite you and Peter to my house again to meet Dame Alice and for measuring for your dominoes. Until then I will say goodnight." As Aleister shook Carrie's hand he looked into her eyes and Carrie felt she was already naked, that no secret was hidden from him. She also felt there was an underlying threat there, should she or Peter disobey him. As she drove back to her cottage she felt her head was spinning with all the information and the massive commitment she was preparing for.

Carrie was a legal secretary for a partnership of solicitors in Seaford. She appreciated her job but she didn't enjoy it. Carrie, of course, wanted more power and influence than any secretary could wield. Her job did require her to speak to the clients, take short hand from the solicitors and type all the letters and legal notes, so she did need to be well rested at nights. Carrie was more worried about that, than any other issue with the coven. She may not have liked her job that much but at that point she did need the income. When she arrived home on Sunday night she thought she may not be able to sleep easily with all those thoughts going around in her head. She found a DVD she liked, called Pretty Woman, the story of a poor street girl making good, and climbed in bed with a cold bottle of wine and a glass. It's a good thing she remembered to set her alarm as she was asleep before Richard Gere had even bought Julia Roberts her new expensive clothes.

She got home from work late Monday evening and had just finished her cheese salad when the front-door bell rang. She invited Peter in and offered him a glass of her white wine, which he gladly accepted and poured herself one too. She thought the evening might be a struggle but Peter seemed to have come to terms with the idea of the dedication and was positive with the arrangements. Truth was Peter had thought about nothing else and each time he thought about it had come back to the realisation that he had nothing going for him in his life and no future as he saw it. He was therefore prepared to gamble his very life for a possible future that promised wealth and influence. At any-rate, sadly, he actually felt that seeing Carrie naked has got to be worth him risking his meagre life. Together, Carrie and Peter started to learn the prayer by heart. They had both realised that the Winter Solstice night was on Sunday which worked out really well as neither of them had to work that day and they could spend the morning preparing for their ceremony and sleep in the afternoon as they had to spend the rest of the night in meditation and prayer. They agreed to get together again on 18th December Thursday evening to make sure they knew the prayer and could remember the routines for the ceremony. However, Aleister telephoned Carrie just as Peter was leaving and asked them both to come to his house at 9pm on Wednesday. They needed to get measured for the dominoes. They both wondered if it was coincidence that Aleister rang just as they were both together. They both decided quite scarily that it was no coincidence. Peter and Carrie then decided to get together after they left Aleister's house on Wednesday evening. As before, Peter could follow Carrie home and go on from there afterwards. Peter left feeling positive and Carrie decided on an early night.

As Aleister put the phone down after ringing Carrie, it rang almost immediately and it was Tamsin, one of the coven members. Tamsin was the aunt of a young girl called Gwendoline. Gwendoline was an Irish girl from Armagh, Northern Ireland who had lost both her parents in a car crash when she was only 3 years of age. A local Roman Catholic Childrens' Home had taken her in and Gwendoline had been brought up by the nuns. In the last few months the Childrens' Home had been desperately searching all the records for any of Gwendoline's surviving family and finally came up with Jenifer O'Brian this English aunt in Lewes (known by the coven members as Tamsin). The Home had to discharge Gwendoline as she was now 16 years of age and according to their rules was no longer a child. Tamsin had talked about this issue at length with Aleister and Dame Alice. It was a massive blessing as the Candlemass celebration required the sacrifice of a sixteen year old virgin. Tamsin had had to check out Gwendoline which had involved her making delicate but thorough checks in respect of Gwendoline. The Childrens' Home wasn't suspicious though, as they were asking Tamsin to take legal responsibility for a 16 year old girl she had never met. The result of the enquiries was that Gwendoline had been cared for and closely protected by nuns since her arrival at the Childrens' Home at 3 years of age. There was no doubt that Gwendoline was still a virgin. Tamsin, Dame Alice and Aleister all believed without doubt that this girl was a timely gift provided by Satan, to enable his worshippers to celebrate Candlemass in his honour.

However the gift of Gwendoline was not without problems, hence the phone call from Tamsin. Gwendoline was arriving on this Saturday 20th December. The irony being that the Childrens' Home wanted Gwendoline settled in with her aunt before Christmas so the child would experience Christmas in her new home. Tamsin had phoned Aleister for guidance as she didn't want to scare the child immediately she arrived but of course neither Tamsin nor any of her friends celebrated Christmas. This young lady will be expecting a tree and Christmas carols!

Following Tamsin's initiation nearly five years ago, Dame Alice had been her guide and teacher. As part of her training Dame Alice had explained the religious history of Britain to widen Tamsin's understanding. She had explained how prior to the Romans arriving in Britain for the second time nearly 2000 years ago, the British peoples were Celts and worshipped the Pagan Gods. The Celts were farming people and their lives revolved around the four seasons, spring, summer, autumn and winter. Their calendar was a circle as the sun and moon where circles and life is a circle; birth, growth, fertility, progeny and death. This circular calendar was then divided into the four seasons and then divided again for the equinoxes, the shortest and longest days, making eight divisions and eight celebrations throughout the year. Yule, which means wheel, is at the top of the calendar and their celebration is called Yuletide.

The Pagan Celts often celebrated Yuletide around a tree, normally an apple tree. The five sided star (Pentacle) is a sacred sign to Pagans and if you cut an apple in half across the middle you will see a five sided star or pentagram. This is why the apple and apple tree are sacred to Pagans. At Yuletide the Pagans celebrated by tying gifts onto the tree. Each Pagan ties onto the tree a miniature scroll with a ribbon around it which has a deep and serious wish written inside, such as the wish for long healthy life, or the wish for a loving partner, or the wish for beautiful healthy children or the wish for an abundant crop that summer. They put the name of the intended on the outside of this scroll. On Yuletide eve they circle the tree and give out their gifts.

When the Romans conquered Britain, from their experiences of previous occupations, they had already learnt that it was easier to control a nation if they could control their religion. When Constantine the Great became a Christian on his death bed, as the emperor was believed to be a God the Romans followed his example and forsook Paganism and turned to Christianity. They therefore wanted the Celts to also worship Jesus. They allowed the Celts to continue celebrating Yuletide with their tree and presents as long as they now called it the Mass for Christ and they were celebrating the birth of Jesus. Which explains why this celebration is at the wrong time of the year for Christ's birth.

Although the Satanists believed the foregoing they strongly opposed Paganism as contrary to Satanism because most Pagans don't believe in Satan as a deity and most Pagans believe Satanism is evil. Nevertheless the Satanists can accept and often do celebrate Yuletide as it is purely celebrating a time of the year, Winter Solstice. Aleister therefore told Tamsin to get a Yuletide tree, which has bare branches and resembles an apple tree in winter. It is nevertheless a tree and she should hang lights and presents on it. With good food and cheerful company Gwendoline will be satisfied. So this is what Tamsin planned for the young girl. Aleister also told Tamsin to bring Gwendoline around to his house on Saturday evening after she arrives. Aleister wanted to make sure he had his eye on this young lady from the time of her arrival.

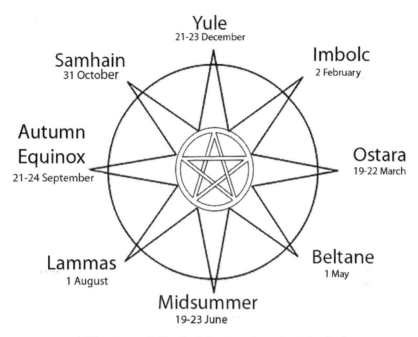

The Pagan Wheel of the Year (Yearly Calendar).

It would actually make more sense for Samhain to be at the top of the wheel because it is the Pagan New Year. The Pagan great bearded God 'Odin' was known as 'Jolnir' which in Old Norse is 'The Yule One'. Yule therefore headed the wheel and the word 'Yule' became synonymous with the wheel.

CHAPTER 4

The Preparations

It was Wednesday 17th December and Peter and Carrie had agreed to meet at Aleister's house. They arrived within five minutes of each other. Peter arrived first and noticed that Carrie's little Suzuki wasn't in the parking area. However there was a bright red new Audi TT which he hadn't seen before. Peter climbed the entrance steps and as usual the great doors swung open. The servant nodded to Peter, the first acknowledgement he had got from him and waved Peter towards the lounge doors. As Peter was about to go through into the lounge the entrance doors started to swing open again. Peter turned and saw the servant waiting at the entrance. As Peter watched, Carrie swept in looking radiant. Her long blond hair looked clean and shone in the lights of the large candelabra hanging above. Her dress met every curve of her body. Peter was spellbound. The servant ushered them both into the lounge. As they entered Aleister rose from his seat to greet them. Next to Aleister was a distinguished looking lady who was probably in her late fifties. She also stood up as they entered, to greet them.

Aleister turned back to face the lady and said "I would like to introduce the High Priestess, Dame Alice. Alice I believe you may have noticed Carrie at a meeting and this is Peter a very new member of our flock." Alice stepped forward and offered her hand. Carrie shook it but Peter took Alice's hand and gently kissed the back of her hand. Alice appreciated the gesture and smiled. "Dame Alice" Carrie said, "Are you a Lady of noble birth, if so how do we address you?" "Carrie my dear, how sweet, not at all. Call me Alice. When we are initiated, as you will be quite soon, we take on spiritual names that we know each-other by and which further helps to protect our privacy. These names are chosen by our High Priest and he sometimes chooses the names of famous historical witches, warlocks and sorcerers." "Is that the case for your name, Alice? Is Dame Alice a famous lady in history?" "Yes, absolutely, Carrie. The Lady I have been named after, was a Lady of noble birth as you call it. Her name was Dame Alice Kyleter. She was credited as being the first witch of Ireland. That is certainly not true. There had been many many witches in Ireland before her but Dame Alice was the first one to be tried and condemned for being a witch. Dame Alice was born in Ireland in 1280. A beautiful Irish noble woman who was married four times. The first three husbands died suddenly and mysteriously, so when her last husband became ill and subsequently died, his children accused her of using witchcraft to murder her husbands. She was arrested and charged and brought before Bishop Ossory. But due to Alice's considerable influence she was not only found not guilty but the Bishop himself was arrested. However Alice was later re-arrested and found guilty but her power and friends enabled her to escape. She travelled to England and was reported to have lived there in comfort for many years and died of old age. Now, my young ones, if I can ask you to accompany me, I need to take you to a room at the back and measure you both. We make the dominoes specifically for each member and in your case we only have 4 days in which to do that."

As Dame Alice turned and walked ahead of them Carrie studied this distinguished confident lady. She was tall, nearly six feet, with long jet black hair that Carrie was sure was her true colour. She wore an expensive looking dress that very nearly touched the floor. Carrie also had this strange feeling that although Alice looked, moved and spoke like a lady in her fifties she was very much older than that. In an empty back room Alice took their measurements and noted them down on a pad she had had waiting with a tape measure. It was obvious it was mainly their height that concerned Alice, she probably didn't want anyone tripping over their domino in the middle of a ceremony. When Alice was satisfied she escorted them both back to the entrance doors.

As they arrived in the entrance hall there was no sign of Aleister who had now left the lounge. Alice pressed a button in the hall they hadn't noticed before and the main entrance doors slowly swung inwards. "Don't worry" Dame Alice said "your dominoes will be waiting for you both, in the bathrooms, on 21st December, Winter Solstice". Carrie and Peter walked out into the cold dark night and as the parking lights turned on, they could see their breath. They had both already agreed that Peter would follow Carrie home again and they would practice their prayer and go through the Dedication routine a few more times. They both drove down the long driveway and out into the dark night.

Three nights later, Saturday 20th December, Aleister had two different guests, Tamsin and Gwendoline. Tamsin was rather short and very overweight, while Gwendoline was slim and tall for her age. Tamsin was, of course, very comfortable and very familiar with Aleister's house. Gwendoline however was very nervous despite Tamsin's regular assurances. When Tamsin and Gwendoline came through the grand entrance it certainly didn't help to calm Gwendoline's nerves. It should be remembered that since the age of three, Gwendoline had lived totally within the walls of a nunnery. Even her schooling was carried out within the nunnery. A teacher came in four times a week to give the children basic lessons in maths, English, geography, history and religious knowledge. Gwendoline would not have realised that she received a predominance of religious teaching and the Roman Catholic interpretations of the scriptures were greatly emphasized. Aleister did not waste time. Gwendoline had no reason not to trust him. The nuns had vouched for Tamsin and Tamsin had vouched for Aleister. After Tamsin introduced Aleister, he sat Gwendoline down in a straight backed chair that had been placed in front of his seating position. He asked Gwendoline to hold out her hands and Aleister took gentle hold of them. Aleister told Gwendoline to look deeply into his eyes. Gwendoline did as she was told and virtually immediately became transfixed, looking as though she was in a trance. Aleister spoke softly and gently to Gwendoline for a few minutes. Finally he kissed her on the forehead and she seemed to wake up. Aleister stood and turned towards Tamsin, nodded and smiled and said "She will do nicely Tamsin. She will co-operate with everything but should there be a problem you are to tell me immediately. Immediately, you understand." He said he will now keep an eye on

Gwendoline, her whereabouts and actions. "You can take her back to your home now" Aleister said. "Please give her a small rum every night when she goes to bed, without fail. If she prefers you can put some blackcurrant with it, but make sure she drinks it. After a while increase it to a double. It will help her sleep in her new environment and get her used to the drink, so she will take it without question on the night, with a little something added." Aleister turned and asked Gwendoline to follow Tamsin which she did immediately. Tamsin and Gwendoline made their way back to Tamsin's house in Lewes, through the cold dark night.

The next day broke clear and bright, not a cloud in the sky. It was cold but then it was 21st December, the shortest day of the year, midwinter's day. Aleister stood on his large patio at the rear of the house drinking coffee. He was looking out at his extensive garden but he was actually focusing on the large circular grassed area in the centre. He had chosen to have this house built at this location for one reason. One of his coven members had been given the gift of dousing. This meant he could find water using just two pieces of willow twigs or two lengths of iron rod bent into a ninety degree shape. This wasn't a rare gift, quite a few Pagans and Satanists had the gift, but George was special. He could not only find water, he had the ability to assess how much water and how deep. He was a sensitive. However it wasn't water that Aleister had been interested in, it was the lay lines, the lines of natural power. Most dousers can find water and also find lay lines but can't differentiate between them, let alone tell you how much water or how much power was in the lines. George could.

When Aleister decided to have a new grander house built he sent George to every large plot of land that was for sale to check it out. When George eventually found this site he came running to Aleister and could hardly speak he was so excited. Approximately four hundred yards from the roadway was a place where two extremely powerful lay lines crossed. It was perfect, a gift from Satan. They could set a large house back from the road far enough to have total privacy and draw their circle behind the house for added secrecy. That place, Aleister was now proudly looking at, where the power lines crossed, was in the centre of the large grass circle, where now stood the large metal cauldron. He was sad though, as they would normally have their Mid-Winter Solstice celebration outside on that circle and dance sky-clad under the moon, an amazing feeling of freedom and natural power. It was a shame especially as the weather was so good. He did briefly consider moving the celebration outside after the dedications but it would have meant closing that circle and opening a new circle outside. Cleansing the area, lighting the cauldron and candles, and calling the four corners took time and concentration but moving the coven members themselves without contamination, from one circle to another is not something to even contemplate. "No, he must put the coven's needs first," Aleister thought "there will be other times."

During the afternoon Aleister took Rachel aside and sat down with her to have a serious chat with her. Rachel was Hungarian. She had had a very unhappy childhood. She had been bullied and beaten by her parents since she was a toddler. Aleister had met her on his travels. She had been a temporary waitress at a café in Paris and had waited on Aleister. Aleister had immediately recognised her past abuse and frailty and he also noticed she hardly spoke at all. She would prefer to nod or shake her head if that was sufficient and then Aleister realised why. She had a bad lisp and occasionally stammered as well, both probably symptoms of her physical abuse. However she was a hard worker and an efficient waitress. She was also still young at 29 and easy on the eye, as they say. When Rachel had come to his table to serve him he had looked deeply into her eyes and Rachel was his.

Back in England the builders had recently finished building the new house at Bridlington so Aleister brought Rachel back from Paris. He familiarised her with her duties at The Pinnacle, which was basically anything Aleister asked her to do. Rachel however was fairly happy at The Pinnacle as she wasn't bullied or beaten by Aleister, and as she was Aleister's, the staff were friendly to her and treated her with respect. She also had her own room, close to Aleister's private rooms. She had no major worries as long as she did what Aleister said and didn't want to go outside the house and grounds or speak to any strangers. Rachel's past was such that she preferred to stay inside and on her own. This was exactly what Aleister had seen in her. Aleister sat Rachel down and explained about Gwendoline. Aleister explained that, as Rachel had been when she first arrived at The Pinnacle, Gwendoline would be very nervous and even frightened. She only knew Tamsin and Tamsin had to leave Gwendoline alone for the whole night whilst they all celebrated. Aleister said that when Tamsin and Gwendoline arrive this evening he will tell Tamsin to introduce her to Gwendoline. Rachel must then ignore all other duties and stay with and look after Gwendoline. She can do what she wants with Gwendoline as long as they both stay inside the house and she does not leave Gwendoline on her own, not even for one second. They must not on any account come into the Temple. Rachel nodded.

Aleister then explained "Gwendoline always has a rum drink as she goes to bed. She must have that every night without fail. I will tell Castor to put two drinks in your room this evening. When Gwendoline becomes tired you both can retire to your room. Make sure Gwendoline has her drink. You can have one as well if you wish. Normally as you know, no-one except myself can enter your room. Tonight is an exception and Gwendoline can rest or sleep with you. Is that all clear?" Rachel nodded and quietly said "Yes." Aleister stood up and left.

***A ceremonial knife and sword known as Athames
can be clearly seen on this pagan altar.

For Aleister, the rest of the afternoon and early evening was taken up with making sure the servants knew what was happening and were preparing enough food and drink for the night ahead. He also made sure that all the magickal impedimenta were clean and in place in the Temple. It included many candlesticks and candles of several colours, mainly black, red, green, blue and yellow. These were used on the altar and the four points of the compass around the circle. It also included a dagger with a curved blade known as a Boline, several beautifully carved pointed sharp knives of different lengths called Athames, and cups and chalices with inverted pentagrams engraved on them. There were wands known as Moon Wands made from different woods; ash, walnut, blackthorn, cherry, oak and ivy. There were three Besom brooms, these were associated with the tree of life. They had hazel wood shafts and the bristles were birch twigs. There was a book of shadows and several books of spells together with a wonderful collection of books on black magick and the black arts. More recent books included 'The Book of Law' by Aleister Crowley, 'Aradia Gospel of the Witches' by Charles Leland and 'The Mystical Qabalah' by Dion Fortune considered one of the best of the more recent books in magick. But Aleister also had four books considered to be the classics of Black Magick; Grimorium Verum by Joseph H. Peterson, De Occulta Philosophia by Cornelius Agrippa, The Grimoire of Pope Honorius considered to be the most important Black Magick Grimoire to come out of France in the 18th century and The Clavicule of Solomon (The Key of Solomon) which appeared to be an original English/Latin version of 1572!

Aleister prepared the altar which stood at the northern end of the circle, as it should. The altar was a marble slab on sculpted marble legs and was very strong. It measured two and a half feet high, two and a half feet wide and six and a half feet long. He placed a black altar cloth over the Altar which had a large inverted pentagram on the top and three large symbols on the cloth where it hung down in front of the altar. On the left was The Sigil of Baphomet, in the centre was The Sigil of Satan and on the far right was The Sigil of Astaroth. 'The Book of Shadows' was placed open at the page for Dedications, on a stand at the back, in the centre of the Altar. Large black candles in black candlesticks stood either side of this book. Aleister then put in place an inverted cross, a Chalice, a Tibetan Singing Bowl, two incense holders and a box of frankincense and myrrh incense sticks, two small glass jars (for the blood samples), two further small glass bowls which will have water in one and salt in the other. All the candlesticks, cups and bowls had inverted pentagrams engraved upon them. He placed a wand, a large ceremonial Athame and two small very sharp Athames (to draw blood). He placed a further black candle in a black candlestick on a gold plate, two old fashioned quill pens, a box of plasters, two small black face-clothes and finally two boxes of matches, at the front of the altar.

It is absolutely essential that everything that is needed for the ceremony is inside the circle because once the corners have been called and the circle closed, it is not appropriate to break the circle and go outside. This rule does of course depend upon the type of celebration or working that is happening in the circle, in some cases such as invoking demons, breaking the circle can even be fatal. Aleister's many years of experience ensured that every item needed was in its right place. He only had to put water in one small bowl on the Altar and salt in another to complete his preparations. He could now go and rest until his guests arrived.

By nine thirty that evening the darkness had already closed in, it was the shortest day of the year, and the temperature had dropped even further as the first members arrived. As Tamsin and Gwendoline came through the great entrance doors, Castor the doorman held out a small ceramic bowl to Tamsin. It was for Yuletide eve. Castor would do the same for everyone who was initiated and invited for Yuletide as they would all have to take a name to prepare their gift. Castor noticed that Tamsin was breathing heavily as she dipped into the bowl. The entrance steps had made her breathless. Aleister also noticed and thought she should be on a diet, as he escorted them into the lounge. Gwendoline had no such problem with the steps but did look very nervous.

Aleister sent for Rachel and when she arrived he introduced her to Gwendoline and reminded Rachel that she was responsible for Gwendoline's welfare and contentment and that she must not go into the Temple under any circumstances. Rachel must also ensure Gwendoline had her bed time drink. Rachel took Gwendoline by the hand and immediately took her off to the staff's play and relaxation room. Rachel thought they may find a DVD Film they would both enjoy. At that moment Peter came into the lounge. Aleister turned, saw Peter and introduced him to Tamsin. Peter had no idea what to say, so he asked if Tamsin was named after a famous historical figure, commenting that he had not heard of a great witch called Tamsin. Tamsin happily explained "I am called after Tamsin Blight also known as the 'White Witch of Helstone'. She was born in Cornwall around 1800 and died 1856. She became a great hedgewitch and conjuror. She was known for casting and removing spells and curses, and for summoning and talking with spirits. She became famous for helping farmers by providing herbs and plants to heal their cattle." "What is a hedgewitch Tamsin?" Peter asked. "Well," Tamsin replied, "The Saxon word for witch is 'Haegtessa' which literally means 'Hedge-rider'. It is the old fashioned witch or wise woman or wise man. They sold magickal charms, herbs and potions. They were the midwife, nurse, doctor and pharmacist in ancient times."

As Peter and Tamsin chatted Carrie came into the lounge. Peter looked at his watch and saw it was five minutes to ten and immediately made his way over to Carrie. They greeted each-other and when Carrie spotted Dame Alice they decided to go to her and ask advice. Dame Alice asked if they both had their dedication instructions and their prayer. When they said they had she led the two of them out into the hall and up the stairs to the balcony. They then went through the door and down the long corridor to the gold doors of the Temple. They saw Aleister in the Temple making last minute preparations but he ignored them as they walked through. At the far end of the Temple was a door that led into the toilets and bathrooms.

Dame Alice pointed to a bathroom and said "Your domino is in there Carrie. Everything you need is in there as well. There is a clean gown for you to put on after you have showered. There is a small glass of rum next to the gown. It has a little something in it to help you keep calm and enjoy the ceremony. Finish the drink, you'll still be able to drive home afterwards. Leave the bathroom at exactly 11pm, there is a clock on the wall. Leave the gown and glass behind as you come out of the bathroom. Carry the domino and walk to the edge of the circle in the Temple. Wait until the High Priest tells you to enter, only then put on the domino as you step into the circle. Then follow his instructions."

Dame Alice then turned to Peter. "Your domino is in that bathroom Peter" she said pointing. "Did you get those instructions Peter?" Peter confirmed he had. "Just make sure you both finish your drinks and do not bring your gowns or glasses out of the bathroom. Bring your dominoes but not wear them until you step into the circle, and please don't forget your instruction papers and prayer and join us at 11pm sharp. Finally after the Dedications you will both leave the circle in your dominoes and come back to the bathrooms. Change into your clothes and carry your dominoes. Do not go back into the Temple. Take that door over there" she said pointing "which will take you downstairs and you'll eventually come out into the entrance hall. Go home and meditate and pray to Satan." Dame Alice looked at her two raw recruits, satisfied herself they were ok and went into the Temple.

Dame Alice checked with Aleister that the circle was ready and then went down to see the staff and make sure they were organised. There were three tables on the left side of the Temple as you came in. The staff were to bring food and drink and lay it out on these tables for the coven members, at exactly midnight. There would also be a special drink for each of the coven, except these drinks had an aphrodisiac in them not a tranquiliser like Carrie and Peter's drinks. Dame Alice then went into the lounge to call the other eleven members of that night's coven. They all came back up the stairs carrying their dominoes and walked through the Temple into the bathrooms. They all chose the end bathrooms so as not to un-nerve the new members. They stripped and showered and walked back to the circle and slipped on their dominoes as they stepped into the circle. This was a regular routine and took them five minutes at the most.

Three members picked up the Besom brooms and chanting quietly, swept the circle from the centre outwards. When the coven members were satisfied they formed a circle. The High Priest took the small bowl of water from the Altar and raised it before him, he raised his hand over the water and said "In the name of Satan, I exorcise thee, o creature of water." Dipping his hand into the water he now sprinkled the 'holy water' around the perimeter of the circle deosil 'sunwise'(in clockwise direction). The High Priest then raised the small bowl of salt, placed his hand over the salt and said "May Satan's blessings be upon this creature of salt." He then dipped his hand into the salt and again walked around the circle sprinkling the salt around the perimeter. Four coven members were standing at the compass points signified by the colour of the candles. North is green and represents earth, East is yellow and represents air, South is red and represents fire and West is blue and represents water. The Satanists at these points, one after the other, starting in the East and working deosil, lighted their candles and 'called the corners', which means they called the demons or elementals representing earth, air, fire and water and invited them to their circle and bade them welcome. The High Priest then drew the circle with the ceremonial Athame which meant he pointed the Athame at the circle boundary and again moving deosil starting at the East, he chanted "In the name of Satan, I conjure thee, our circle of power, that thou be a protection and boundary between the worlds." Then lighting the incense sticks and the candles upon the Altar he called upon Astaroth to join them in the circle. The circle was now closed and preparations were complete. It was a few minutes to 11pm.

CHAPTER 5

The Dedications

Peter finished his shower, dried off and put on his gown. He sat sipping his rum drink trying not to imagine what was going to happen. He wanted to just 'go with the flow'. He had heard the coven members all come into the bathrooms and the showers going and the laughter. He had decided he did want to be with them, just wasn't sure he could cope with the trials of getting there. He will probably rely on Carrie and follow her lead. She was more confident than him, had a stronger resolve. He wasn't sure if she had finished her shower yet. He looked at the clock and suddenly realised it was a couple of minutes past 11 pm. He put down his empty glass and jumped up, picked up his papers, stepped outside the bathroom, took off his cloak, and feeling very vulnerable and embarrassed opened and stepped through the door into the Temple. Carrie was ahead of him. She had probably been watching the time more carefully. Carrie was just stepping up to the circle. Peter thought she was as magnificent as he expected, at least she was from behind. Long shapely legs meeting at a perfect bottom, beautiful curves to a long slender neck, partly obscured by her long blond hair hanging down over her right shoulder. Over her left arm hung her long grey domino and in her right hand her papers. On Aleister's instruction she stepped into the circle and pulled her domino over her head. As she went to pull up her hood she looked up and for a second she froze. On the ceiling was a circular Baphomet, the Head of the Goat of Mendes within the inverted Pentagram, the symbol of Satan. But this Baphomet

was in black and shades of grey and something about it made it very
sinister, a Dark Circle. It was immediately above the centre of the
circle. As she reached for and pulled up her hood she shivered. All the
other coven members were facing into the centre of the circle and were
similarly attired with their hoods up, excepting the High Priest and
High Priestess who had bright multicoloured ceremonial gowns on.

Peter was now approaching the circle as well. Aleister turned to
him and invited him in the circle. Peter copied Carrie and stepped
into the circle and slipped his domino on and put up his hood. Aleister
pointed to the centre of the circle and Peter and Carrie moved to
where he had indicated. Aleister looked at Carrie "Do you know the
prayer?" She said "Yes" and nodded. "Please put your hands together,
turn and look upwards at Satan's Dark Circle on the ceiling and recite
your promise." Carrie turned and looked up and clasped her hands in
prayer and said "Before the Almighty God Satan and in the presence
of our patron Demoness Astaroth and the True Original Gods, and
the Elementals representing Air, Fire, Water and Earth, I renounce any
and all past allegiances. I renounce Eostra, and all the Old Pagan Gods,
I renounce the false Christian god Jehova. I renounce his vile and
worthless son Jesus. I renounce his foul, odious and rotten Holy Spirit.
I proclaim Satan as my one and only God. I promise to recognise and
honour him in all things, without reservation, desiring in return, his
bountiful assistance in the successful completion of my desires." Carrie
then bowed her head and went silent.

Peter shivered, he thought it might be his imagination, but it
seemed as though it had suddenly turned cold. Then he noticed that
there was a mist in the smaller circle just the other side of the yellow
candle on the circle perimeter, in the east corner. As he watched
the lights in the Temple dimmed and the mist seemed to be getting
thicker and he could swear there appeared to be a figure forming
in the mist. It was becoming a female form; tall, dark skinned and
virtually naked. Peter wasn't afraid, he was totally transfixed. The
female form was materialising in front of them, the mist clearing
and the temperature dropping further. There was also a quiet sound
of a wind. It was a low whistle as one sometimes hears in a wood on
a windy day. The figure now in front of them was a female warrior,
wearing only a loin cloth and carrying a shield and spear. However

she did not seem to be hostile. She didn't speak, she just looked at each person in turn around the circle, but when she got to Peter her gaze halted and remained briefly on him. The combination of the sound of the wind, the mist, the coldness in the air and this figure of power was awesome and frightening to Peter. She seemed to be assessing him and he felt weak and helpless in her gaze. He was about to collapse when she looked away and Peter recovered enough to remain standing. This Peter assumed was Astaroth. He looked at Carrie who had now raised her head but seemed to be frozen in time. The High Priest then called Peter and told him to recite his prayer but to focus on Astaroth. "Peter," Aleister said "clasp your hands in prayer, look only at Astaroth, do not look away for even a second, it would be disrespectful. Recite your prayer, as Carrie did." Peter did as he was told. At no time did his eyes wander from Astaroth. When he finished his prayer, Aleister said they both must turn towards the altar.

Carrie and Peter turned and found they were facing the High Priest and High Priestess who were standing in front of the Altar. Dame Alice had a small Athame in her hand. Aleister held a black cloth, a small glass and a quill pen. They looked at Carrie first and asked her to hold out her left hand. Dame Alice took her hand, turned it so the index finger was on top and raised the athame and cut the side of the finger. The cut was small and the knife so sharp Carrie hardly felt it. The High Priestess lowered the hand and squeezed the finger. As she did so the High Priest held the glass to catch the blood. The High Priest gave Carrie the cloth to wipe the finger and told her to put her prayer on the altar and sign it. Although the lights had remained dim the large black altar candles gave more than adequate light to see the prayer. Aleister held out the quill pen and the glass with a drop of blood in the bottom. Carrie didn't need to read it as she had already memorised it word for word, so she just dipped the pen in her blood and signed her name. She remembered what she had to do, so she took the signed prayer and held it in the flame of the candle immediately in front of her and once it was burning well she dropped it into the gold plate. When she saw the prayer had been totally burnt she pushed back her hood, looked up and cried "So mote it be" and then with a very loud shout "Hail Satan". As she did so the dim lights flickered and the quiet wind become a roar and everyone's gowns were blown about as though they were in a storm.

Peter found himself thinking 'this is no cult, this is the real thing'. He was elated, as though an electrical charge was running through his body. He couldn't wait to complete his dedication. As the wind calmed, the High Priestess turned and asked for Peter's left hand. Again she turned it so the index finger was upper most and The High Priest gave her the other small athame which she used to make a small cut. The High Priestess lowered the hand and squeezed the finger whilst Aleister held the second glass under the cut. When Aleister gave him the pen Peter turned dipped in into his blood and signed his prayer, then burnt it in the flame. As before when Peter shouted "So mote it be" followed by "Hail Satan" the room erupted into a storm.

It was obvious the High Priest was very pleased with them both. Smiling he told them to go and change, and then to go home and pray to Satan for the rest of the night. "However do not come back into the Temple on your way out." They both left the circle and made their way to the bathrooms. After changing and picking up their papers and dominoes they met, as arranged, outside the bathrooms. Together they took the exit door which led them downstairs into a corridor. They followed the corridor and walked passed several doors, as their instructions stated. At the end of the corridor they opened the door and walked into the entrance hall. They were both in a dreamlike state. They stepped outside and the cold night air helped to 'sober them up'. They needed to be fully awake to drive home. They hadn't spoken a word to each other at that point. Peter broke the silence by firstly just saying "Wow!!" and then "I'll ring you when I get home Carrie, just to check you are ok and got home safely". "Yes, that's fine. Well done Peter you did fine." With that Carrie walked over to her car and the two of them drove out into the night.

As Peter was driving home he remembered Aleister's warning 'Astaroth is my personal Guardian Demoness as High Priest of the coven. Anyone attacking me physically or spiritually may have to face her wroth.' When Astaroth kept her gaze on me for just a few seconds, Peter thought, he had a slight glimpse of the hidden power there. Peter was pretty sure he wouldn't want to face her in a bad mood, let alone her full wroth. However, the idea of having a powerful protector such as Astaroth was very attractive to Peter and on its own, justified what Peter was doing.

In the meantime, back at the circle, preparations were in hand for the Mid-Winter Solstice. When Carrie and Peter left the Temple to go and change, Astaroth had faded back into a mist and the Satanists noticed that the wind had stopped and the Temple had become warm again. By then it was only a few minutes to midnight. The Satanists were relaxing, chatting and laughing but they stayed within the confines of the circle. They were waiting for the servants to bring the refreshments, which arrived exactly at midnight. The servants came into the Temple loaded with plates and bowls of cold meats and fruit, which they arranged onto the tables. They also brought the 13 glasses of rum that had an aphrodisiac added, and bottles and glasses for different types of wines and spirits. The nearest table that had their special drinks was carefully located so that they could reach their drinks without leaving the circle. Once the servants had left, the members reached over and took the drinks and passed them around to their colleagues. When everyone had their drink they all, including the High Priest and High Priestess, came to the centre of their circle and clashed their glasses together laughing and shouting in celebration and swallowed the drink. They passed back the empty glasses and returned to their position on the circle.

The High Priest could now look about the Temple as the lights had returned to normal. Happy that all the food and drink had been delivered and all the servants had left, he shouted "Hail Satan" and pulled off his ceremonial robe and dropped it in the circle but at the very edge. The High Priestess then did the same; shouting "Hail Satan" and removed her robe. The eleven Satanists immediately copied their masters and also linked hands, leaving the High Priest and High Priestess in the centre of the circle. The High Priest then said "We have completed our working tonight, but before we celebrate the Mid-Winter Solstice I want us to further increase the power of the energy in the aura of our circle."

Aleister had picked up the Singing Bowl from the Altar and now passed it to Dame Alice. As he did so he said "For the benefit of George, our newest member here, I'll explain that these bowls are believed to have originated in Tibet possibly 15th century and are a type of standing bell. They can be struck with the mallet like any hanging bell but our High Priestess will stroke the rim with the mallet to make it 'sing'. As she does so imagine Astaroth standing in front of you in the middle of the circle. Pour your concentration and psychic energy into the centre of the circle where Astaroth stands. The combined power of you all, will create a cone of power and as you feel this power rise, move your centre of concentration upwards until it is focused on the Dark Circle above." The High Priest nodded at Alice.

Dame Alice picked up the mallet and slowly and gently moved the leather capped end of the mallet around the rim. It started to hum and Alice increased the speed slightly until the bowl was 'singing'. All the Satanists were facing towards the centre of the circle, some were looking at the floor in the centre and some had their eyes closed concentrating. The bowl continued to sing and some of the Satanists joined in humming. Very slowly the Satanists started to sway with the rhythm of the singing bowl and the sound of the bowl and the humming began to build up and the electricity in the air increased. George had his eyes open at first but found he was distracted by the naked bodies swaying. As some of them were overweight it was more comical than sensual. So he closed his eyes and then felt he could see sparks coming off some of the members. He must have been imagining it, he thought, as his eyes were tightly closed now. After approximately ten minutes all the members were concentrating on the Dark Circle on the ceiling, and George felt that he could feel and nearly touch the power and energy in the circle. He hadn't done this Coning of power before. The High Priestess then started to slow down the 'singing' bowl and the members began to stop humming and swaying, until all was quiet and still.

George opened his eyes and was immediately surprised to see two of the male Satanists had hard erections. He didn't know if this was normal with this ritual. Aleister noticed George's reaction and smiled and said "Let me explain that Coning power means that we use our minds and bodies to generate power and funnel it to a central point so that the collective power of the coven is unified. This power is coursing through our bodies and affects us all differently. One of these effects can be that the increased physical stimulation increases our blood flow and that often causes erections. It is a very good sign. It means that our attempts to generate this aura of power were successful. I am sure our lady members will reward these successful 'members' later." This comment was accompanied by a few giggles. "In case anyone doesn't know there is a special connection between Astaroth and Coning. The Phoenician worshippers of Astaroth, working with her, developed the art of Coning power. So much so, that Astaroth became known for it and the Cone became her emblem. This comes from the circle of power building up to a point at the top. In writings and drawings her followers were seen with this Cone. The Black Cone became her emblem. Many years later witches were depicted as wearing these Cones and the myth of the witches hat was born. The general public still think of witches as wearing these pointed hats and not cloaks and hoods, as we do. Enough education, let us celebrate the Mid-Winter Solstice. Hail Satan" and they all shouted their approval.

The High Priest thanked Satan for his presence and protection, and then thanked Astaroth for her presence and protection and especially for showing herself. Aleister then asked the 'corners' to open the circle. They naturally started at the north, Earth, thanked the elementals, blew out the candle and then went widdershins (counter-clockwise) doing the same in turn around the circle, finishing at the east, the yellow candle representing Air. The circle open and ceremony complete there was then a great rush to the tables and they started to consume the food and drink as though they had starved for weeks. George found himself looking at the female members with sudden interest and noticed that the other members were fondling each-other even as they ate. Obviously, he thought, either this Coning affects everyone in that way or the aphrodisiac is kicking in. Within an hour most of the food and drink had been consumed and everyone was drunk and had slated their lust. The exception being the High Priest and High Priestess who remained in control, basically so they can organise the staff to take these eleven revellers to their rooms for the night. The High Priestess would take one of the male members to her room if she had the need but resisted it that night. The High Priest had to perform sexual intercourse, actual penetration, as part of all new initiations and sacrifices and didn't see it as pleasure. He would go to Rachel to meet his needs. By 3am everyone had been taken to a room and was asleep or passed out.

Monday morning broke clear and bright but cold, but then it was 22nd December. The staff had been up some time organising a buffet breakfast in the dining hall downstairs. They had knocked on everyones' doors, as requested, at 9am, telling the guests breakfast was in the dining hall. Very slowly the guests appeared over the next two hours. The coffee urn was topped up with fresh coffee several times. When Aleister walked in George was helping himself to the orange juice and Aleister joined him. "I guess you understand now why we couldn't have the celebrations outside?" Aleister said. "Not really, please explain" George replied. "Dedications are really important and Astaroth likes to attend, which is wonderful, but as well as fertility and motherhood she is also the Demoness of War so she is often accompanied by a great wind which creates havoc outside if we are doing something delicate such as taking blood for a Dedication. I also like the new members to concentrate on the Dark Circle on the ceiling above us when they are making their promise. That is why I like to have Dedications in the Temple. It is then very difficult, if not dangerous, to try and transfer to another circle outside. Satan willing, we will be able to celebrate outside soon." George nodded, Aleister smiled and walked over to the cereals where Margaret was helping herself. "Aleister" Margaret said "That's the new coven member called George, isn't it?" "Yes that's right Margaret" "Can I ask you Aleister, who you have named him after?" "George has been with the group now for two years, so he isn't that new to us but you are right, this is only his second time in the circle. George is named after George Pickingill who was born in Essex. He was credited with reforming witchcraft and forming nine covens. He became a part of the Hermetic Order of the Golden Dawn but was later thrown out because of his allegiance to Satan and Black Magic. As you know Margaret, everyone in the circle is blessed with at least one gift to support the coven, and George is the greatest dowser I have ever worked with. It is because of George that we have this powerful circle here. Excuse me Margaret I have to talk to Dame Alice and Dr John".

Aleister had seen Dame Alice and Dr John eating breakfast quietly away from the others, at the far end of the room. Aleister walked over to them and sat down at the table. "I hope you guys don't mind me sitting at your table?" Aleister said. Dr John smiled "But it's your table Aleister." "But only because of you Dr John" Aleister replied. Then looking at Dame Alice he said "Seriously, I need you to spend time with Peter and Carrie, check they are alright and start preparing them for initiation. I suggest you invite them here for 9pm Wednesday. You must tell them that we are celebrating Yuletide with sexual rituals that night so they cannot join in or stay beyond 11pm as they are not initiated yet." "I will organise that after breakfast Aleister" Dame Alice replied. Aleister switched his attention back to Dr John, "I need to have a meeting with you and we need to look at future movements in the markets as some of the stocks seem unstable. Can you come round tomorrow evening when we shouldn't be disturbed." "Of course Aleister" Dr John replied and Aleister stood up, nodded at them both and left the dining hall.

Castor, Aleister's doorman, had been spending time preparing for Yuletide evening. He had found a small but attractive apple tree, bare branched of course, it was December, and he had had it planted in a beautiful ceramic tub in the centre of the entrance hall so the guests would be able to stand around it in two days time. There were stars, pentagrams (upright and inverted), shiny bright red artificial apples and sparkling lights hanging from the branches. A gold inverted pentagram was on the top. It looked beautiful. On Wednesday night all the guests would arrive with a gift; a small scroll of paper with a wish written on the inside, a name on the outside and a bow. As they came into the entrance hall they would each hang their gift on the tree. All the guests from the night before, admired the tree as they finally left the house and one or two who had been missed out asked Castor for a name from the bowl. As Dame Alice was leaving she saw Aleister and told him that Carrie was at work but she would speak to her and Peter tonight.

CHAPTER 6

An Uninvited Visitor

It was Wednesday 24th December, for Christian children the best night of the year. It often was for Pagan children as well, because the children would feel 'hard done by' if they didn't get presents as well. So their Pagan parents would give them presents, toys that is and not just spiritual good wishes as Pagan tradition is supposed to be. It was another cold but clear night as Carrie and Peter arrived at The Pinnacles. This time they arrived together. They had agreed that Peter would come to Carrie's house and then they would come on from there in Carrie's car. They were pleased they had come in one car as there were a lot of cars parked in front of the house that night. Peter noticed that the expensive cars he had seen before were all there. Obviously the entire membership had been invited.

As they came into the entrance hall they stood and looked at the tree which looked beautiful. Castor had turned down the dimmer switch that controlled the chandelier, so the lights on the tree seemed much brighter and sparkled off the tree ornaments and the many pretty little scrolls tied up with coloured ribbon hanging from the branches. Each guest had hung a Yuletide scroll on the tree when they arrived. Castor waited patiently whilst Carrie and Peter admired the tree and when they were ready escorted them into the lounge. Considering the number of guests Carrie and Peter expected to hear a high level of background noise but there were no sounds of talking or laughter. The coven was obviously going to celebrate outside under the moon and stars. Carrie and Peter both wished they could join them.

When they walked into the main lounge they saw Dame Alice who was obviously expecting them. Dame Alice had just poured herself a drink and offered them one as well. Even though they were now car sharing they both had to drive, so declined. After Castor had left and the three of them had made themselves comfortable, Dame Alice welcomed them back and said "Your Dedications really went very well. You were very privileged and blessed, Astaroth was not only present, she showed herself to you both. Carrie you told me that you are both happy with moving on to your initiations. As I think you know we wouldn't normally move this quickly but we have a special purpose for you Carrie and a very short time frame. I now have the responsibility to advise and educate you both so you understand what initiation is all about and what you are committing to. Tonight I will explain a few basics and then we can get together a few more times before the big night.

Now the big night: in your case is St. Winebald's Day. We celebrate this on 7th January. It is important you understand about this day, as it will be life changing in your case. Let me tell you the story of St. Winebald. He was born about 700 AD in what was then Wessex in England. He had two brothers and a sister. He became a Benedictine Abbot and went on a pilgrimage to Rome and the Holy Land with one of his brothers and his father. His father died in Lucca and the two brothers went onto Rome. He studied in Rome for seven years before returning to England. He later gathered together a group of missionaries and went to Germany where he was ordained in 739 AD. He struggled against the local Pagans but made the monastery he founded one of the leading Christian centres in Germany. He died in 768 AD on 18th December which became his feast day of remembrance."

"Excuse me," Carrie said "but you said his celebration day is 7th January?" "And so I did Carrie." Alice replied "In the 1970s in London the Metropolitan police were having a 'crack down' on Satanic covens and kept raiding them when they were having their ceremonies or celebrations. The covens started feeding the police with false information so their raids were unsuccessful. The police were led to believe that on St. Winebald's day we had human sacrifices and the celebration was on 7th January. This totally disrupted their raids which were heavily focused on the wrong day and shortly afterwards the raids were stopped. St. Winebald's Day became known by everyone as 7th January and eventually the Roman Catholics and Satanists accepted this new date as his remembrance day."

"So how is it that both the Roman Catholics and Satanists celebrate this man?" Peter asked. "From what I understand," replied Alice "the Roman Catholics celebrate his devotion and inspiration in establishing the most successful monastery in Germany in the 8th century, whilst Satanists who are unhappy about his persecution of Pagan beliefs desecrate his Memory by having initiations, animal sacrifice and sexual rituals on his day of remembrance. We don't have a great deal of time tonight so I will allow each of you one further question about the coven."

"Can you explain the robes, in respect of the colours?" Carrie asked. "We are in single colours whilst the High Priest and yourself wear multiple colours. Are these colours significant?" "All covens are a little different with respect to robes" Dame Alice replied "some don't even wear them and are skyclad all the time they are in the circle. The principle is that nothing dirty or contaminated from this world must go into the sacred space. It is a matter of protection for us and a matter of respect to Astaroth and Satan. The robes must not be worn outside the circle and must be thoroughly washed between wearings. Now in respect of the colours: some covens have three colours, one colour for members that haven't been initiated, a second colour for initiates and then multi colours for Priests and Priestesses. This coven requires you to be initiated before you can fully join the circle so we have just two colours. One colour for initiates and multicoloured for Priests. At the moment we don't have any Priests other than the High Priest and myself. The initiates are required to be grey but the Priests can choose any combination of different colours. The Status is signified by being multicoloured not the specific colours. As in the Bible, when they wanted to degrade and destroy Joseph they stripped him of his coat of many colours, same principle. The story refers to Joseph's coat and it being many colours because it is a significant status."

"Can I ask Dame Alice, how is it we can only have thirteen in the circle but our membership must be twice that. How does it work?"

Peter asked. "Very simply Peter, as you say we have to have thirteen in the circle for any magickal workings, so if we only had thirteen members if someone is sick it would disrupt the coven. We therefore have several more members than we need to create a circle. When we are doing strict worship, ritual or magickal workings the High Priest chooses the members to assist in the circle; so this is a privilege, an honour for those that are chosen. He does try to give everyone experience in the circle though. However when we are celebrating outside under the stars for Mid-Winter, Summer Solstice or Yuletide for example, then every initiate is invited. Does that answer your question Peter?" "Yes, thank you, Dame Alice." Dame Alice then said "It is now 10.30 and we start Yuletide celebrations at 11 pm. I therefore need to draw our little session to a close and escort you both to the entrance. By the way, there is nothing to stop you both having your own Yuletide celebration at home." With that Dame Alice arose and escorted them to the front doors. "Happy Yuletide, Hail Satan" she said as they stepped out into the cold night.

As Carrie drove back to her cottage Peter was wondering if Carrie would ask him if he wanted to stay, even if it was a separate room it would be nice so he could have a few drinks. Hell, it is Christmas eve. Carrie didn't. In fact as they climbed out of her car she said "I am not going to ask you to stay Peter, even if it is Yuletide or Christmas eve. I don't want any emotional entanglements within the coven. Please don't read anything into it. Its not really personal, its just the way I want it. Is that ok with you?" "Of course, I'll see you again when Dame Alice contacts us about our next teach in." Peter jumped in his car and drove back to his flat. He wasn't really expecting anything else so he wasn't that disappointed. He watched a terrible old Christmas film and was about to go to bed when the phone rang.

He was a little surprised and concerned as it was nearly midnight and it may mean it was a distressing call. Far from it, it was Liz, Elizabeth Shipton to be more accurate. "Hi Peter, I hope I haven't woken you up?" "No you haven't. Just finished watching the worst film of all time. I have got to ask what has happened to make you call me at midnight on Christmas eve?" "Nothing really Peter. I was very sad when you and Sue broke up and then you moved out and when I enquired at 'Foster & Shilling' Estate Agents you weren't working there anymore, so I lost track of you. Then I bumped into Steve, you know Pagan Steve, he admitted he knew where you were now but refused to tell me. He was very funny, funny weird that is. Have you had a row the two of you? Anyrate I then met Cathy and she said she saw you working in that 'Bright Mornings' café on the corner. I called in there this morning, they said it was your day off but agreed to give me a contact number. I had to finish a photo shoot this evening as it had to be done by Christmas and only just got back to my flat. Found myself thinking about you a lot recently. What are you doing for Christmas?" "Actually I'm not doing anything and not doing it with anyone. I've been on my own since Sue and I broke up. I joined a circle of friends to make me feel better about myself. They are helping and I'm feeling much better but I still haven't had one date. I think I'm over Sue now but just need to meet the right girl." "Look Pete, I know how this must sound but how about you coming over and joining me tomorrow. I'm on my own as well, Mark and I split up weeks ago and I don't think anyone should be on their own at Christmas." "That is a great idea Liz, are you still in the flat at 3 Reginald Crescent?" said Peter. "Yes, Mark moved out, after I found out he was two timing me." "Oh, not nice. What time do you want me there?" Liz thought about it for a minute, then said "How about noon?" "I've got no card or pressie for you though," Peter said "What do you want me to bring?" "Just yourself Peter and a nice bottle of wine if you have one." "I'll see you at noon Liz, Happy Christmas."

Christmas morning broke wet and windy. No chance of snow then, Peter thought. Still he was happier than he had been for some time. He showered and shaved and even caught himself singing Christmas carols. Hell he thought I'm a Satanist now, singing Christian carols. It didn't seem to worry him though. After a good breakfast he went and found his car; often couldn't remember where he parked it as it's in a different place every time. However by the time he was in the car he was very wet. It had started to rain again and he hadn't brought an umbrella. Then he went hunting for a shop that was open. Brighton is good like that. So cosmopolitan with so many religions there is always a shop open no matter what day of the year. He soon found a corner shop he could park outside which sold a small selection of nearly everything. He bought a Christmas card, a box of chocolates, a bottle of

Baileys Irish Liqueur and a bottle of wine from a town in Spain he had never heard of. He was about to leave the shop when he noticed that behind the till there was a board displaying a selection of necklaces. They didn't look too bad, at least not from that distance. He chose one and asked the man to wrap it in Christmas paper he also bought.

When he got back into his car, he opened the card and wrote in it 'As I've had too many clouds I am hoping you are my silver lining, all my love, Peter.' He drove on to Newhaven and struggled to find Reginald Crescent, as he had only gone to Liz's flat once and that had been with Sue, more than two years ago. Peter still arrived half an hour early and hoped Liz wouldn't mind. When Liz opened her front door her smile showed she wasn't unhappy. She looked much the same as Peter remembered. A little chubbier maybe but her pretty face and big hazel eyes were still very attractive. She kissed Peter on the cheek as he came in and Peter walked through to the kitchen where he put down his shopping. Liz came up behind him and helped him off with his wet raincoat. He passed her the drink and chocolates and then gave her the card and present. She opened the card, read it, smiled and said "That's up to you" then turned and gave him a very strong hug. He could feel that hug could become much more if he wanted but she let go and opened her little present. He got another enthusiast hug and when she reluctantly let go she said "And how the Hell have you got these, are you psychic? You didn't know you were coming here until midnight last night. I haven't got you anything." "Remember I live in Brighton," Peter said "there is always a shop open. The Muslim shop owners are open at Christmas, it's a great opportunity for them. Anyrate those cuddles were better than any present." Liz smiled, turned and put the bottle of white wine in the fridge and then took his hand and walked him into the lounge.

"You OK with Christmas TV?" She said as she sat on the sofa and patted the seat next to her. Peter made himself comfortable and they watched the Christmas programmes and chatted. "That white wine should be chilled enough now" Liz said and jumped up and went into the kitchen. "One glass before dinner eh?" Peter smiled and nodded and took the glass she held out. "I have a confession Peter" Liz said. "OK what is it?" Peter replied thinking that by her serious voice it was going to be a big deal. "Are you OK with ready cooked Christmas dinner? I had no intention of cooking a full Christmas dinner just for myself so I bought those ready cooked ones. I've had them before and they are fine. I bought two meals when I went to the shops a couple of days ago. I don't know what I was thinking though. Was that for Christmas day and Boxing day or was that habit of buying for two from my days with Mark? When you said you weren't doing anything today I immediately thought of the two Christmas meals. You alright with that?" "Very much. I have the feeling this could turn into one of my best Chritmas dinners, certainly in the last two years." Peter replied. "While I'm in the kitchen do you want to lay the table, I'm sure you can find everything? Just shout if you can't." When Peter had finished with the table layout he went into the kitchen. Liz was opening a tin of carrots and peas and putting them in a saucepan. "I am trying to enhance our ready made meals" she said. Peter came up behind Liz and put his arms around her waist and gave her a cuddle. When her hands were free she held his two hands and slid them upwards so he was holding her breasts. He caressed her breasts and then she turned in his arms and kissed him on the lips, soft and gentle but with promise. "I think we need to have dinner I've already heated it up" she said, as she gently pushed him away, turned and finished the preparations. "Take the bottle in and put it on the table, I put it back in the fridge." He reluctantly let go and did as she asked.

After dinner Liz again took Peter's hand and still with a glass of wine in her other hand led him upstairs to her bedroom. "I haven't got a TV in my bedroom Peter" she said "Are you going to be OK missing the Queen's speech?" "I got the feeling it's not going to be a great loss" Peter replied.

Later they lay and chatted for a while and then slept for an hour or so. Peter thought Liz looked really content but he was still restless. Liz began to notice his mood and asked him what the problem was. "Don't misunderstand my mood Liz. That was beautiful, you are beautiful. I could easily fall in love with you. It's my mother" he said. "Last Christmas my mother was still alive and she joined Sue and I for Christmas. I am just sad I can't talk to her." "Do you believe in life after death Peter?" "Yes I think I do Liz. In fact, I am not allowed to talk about it, but I'm sure it's OK just to tell you I have joined a coven recently." "Ah, is that Steve's coven?" "No, its not and Steve didn't approve of the one I joined, which is why he was funny with you, when you asked after me. Why did you ask about me believing in life after death?" "Well, you were talking about missing your mother and missing talking to her. I have an Ouija board also called a Spirit board. Have you ever used one?" "No" Peter replied "I have heard of them but I don't know anything about them. Do they really work?" "Well they all say that it depends on the person or people using it. We can give it a try if you want. It would be nice if you heard from your mother on Christmas day, wouldn't it?" "Making love with you and contacting my mother would make this the best Christmas ever. Yeah, go for it, the board I mean."

It was getting dark by then, so Liz and Peter closed the curtains and cleared the table. Liz collected the board and planchette, turned the lights down low, got two candles, a box of incense sticks and a holder. She put a writing pad and pencil on the table. Then she lit the candles and incense for atmosphere and they settled at the table with recharged wine glasses. "What's the name of this again Liz?" "The Board is called an Ouija board. It comes from the French and German words for yes, that is Qui and Ja. The word 'Planchette' is the French word for 'little plank', which of course it is. Some people say the Ouija board and planchette date back thousands of years but in fact it was invented as a game in 1890 by Elijah Bond. I looked it up at the library out of interest. For many years it was just a game but then in about 1915 a well respected spiritualist called Pearl Curran said the board can be used to find missing objects or people or can be used to contact the spirits of dead people. The board sold in the thousands as it was being used by Americans trying to find or contact family who were fighting in the First World War."

"OK, thank you, that's very helpful but how do we use it?" Peter said. Liz replied "It is best if only one person is asking the questions that way there is less confusion. So that person is the medium. That should be you as it's your mother we want to contact. That leaves me to be the recorder," and Liz reached for the writing pad and pencil as she said this. "OK," Liz said "rest your index finger on the planchette, we move it together to the 'G,' centre of the board. Now very gently move the planchette around the board in slow circles. This will give us the feel and warm up the board. Now you need to talk to your mother, ask if she is here, ask if she hears you, ask if she is happy. Simple questions she can answer by directing the planchette to yes and no. As you get the feel for it you can ask something your mother has to spell out. I will write down everything the board says. If we don't like the spirit, if we don't think it is your mother we just say goodbye by moving the planchette to the bottom of the board. OK give it a try." With the lights down low Liz couldn't see the writing pad very well so she moved one of the candles closer. The low lights, the smell of the incense and the flickering of the candles did make the atmosphere very 'ghostly'. Liz was now really glad she wasn't doing this on her own.

At first nothing much happened. Peter kept asking if his mother was there, if she could hear him. No response. The planchette continued to go in gentle circles. Then in frustration Peter asked if anyone was there and the planchete seemed to take off across the board to the 'yes'. Both Peter and Liz were shocked and by their faces they didn't cause the movement. He then asked if they knew this spirit. Again it shot over to 'no'. "If we don't know you" Peter said "can you tell us your name?" At that, the planchette became animated, flying around the board. Liz was scared by its reaction and scared that she couldn't record what it said, as it was spelling out words very rapidly. Liz had her head turned down concentrating on the planchette but in the corner of her eye she thought she saw Peter shiver. Once she had noticed that she realised she was cold, the temperature in the room was dropping. The planchette stopped. She looked at her note pad, it said 'D A I M O N'. That is rubbish or she got it wrong. She looked up at Peter and the blood in her face drained, she was suddenly very cold and very scared. There was a dark figure standing behind Peter. She couldn't see a face or any detail, just a black silhouette.

She didn't need to be told this wasn't Peter's mother, this was malevolent. She immediately moved the planchette to 'goodbye' and leapt up and turned on the lights. There was no person, shadow or ghost standing there behind Peter. Peter was of course looking at her in shock. He could see something was very wrong, Liz was as white as a sheet. As the saying goes, she looked like she had just seen a ghost, which was exactly what she thought. She was sure it was connected with Peter because she would have expected to need him to stay the night and keep her company but her instincts were completely different. She immediately wanted him out the flat. Everything in her being was screaming to get him out. She said "Peter I am really sorry but I feel very unwell and need to be on my own. Will you please leave immediately." "Are you sure Liz" he said "you look scared, don't you want me to stay with you, so you are not on your own." "No," she said "I want you to leave right now." She virtually pushed Peter out the living room and towards the front door, he only just had time to grab his coat on the way.

Peter found himself standing outside Liz's flat in the rain on Christmas night and he had no idea why. He shook his head, mumbled a few phases about the unpredictability of women and walked over to his car. He had had no intention of driving home that night and had half the bottle of wine in him on Christmas night. He would really struggle to get a cab tonight so decided to risk the drive home. He found a tube of mints and started sucking them and kept the windows half open despite the rain and cold, in case he did get stopped by the police. He drove home slowly but not too slowly as to draw attention to himself. There were quite a few cars on the road to Brighton so he felt a bit better, and did get home and safely parked.

In the meantime Liz had finished the last of the wine and jumped into bed. She left the bedside lamp on and climbed under the bedclothes. Eventually she fell asleep, probably all the wine but she had an awful dream. A black shape came out of the air and descended on her in the bed. She was pretty sure he raped her and woke up in the morning in a terrible state. She soon realised it was just a dream and considering what happened the night before it is understandable. She staggered into the bathroom to go to the toilet and as she sat down on the toilet her night dress rode up her legs and they were covered in scratches. She screamed and then fell forward shaking. As she calmed a little she realised that her natural reaction which was to call the police was ridiculous. She could hear herself saying 'It's like this Officer I saw a ghost and then had this terrible dream in the night.' No I don't think so, she thought. Then she realised, the only person who could help her and would believe her would be Steve Conners. She climbed back on her feet and rang him. He was in thank God. He quietly listened to what she told him and asked lots of questions. He must have believed her because he said to stay there, don't go out and he will collect his coven's High Priestess and they will be with her as fast as they can. He asked her if she had his mobile number and when she said she did he said that if anything further happened, to ring him immediately, he has hands free in his car.

CHAPTER 7

A Light in the Dark

Steve and Lauren arrived at Liz's flat just under an hour later, which was very fast as Lauren wasn't expecting any of this and had decided on a lie-in on Boxing Day. Also Lauren and Steve had had to get together a few things to bring with them. Lauren brought first aid and nursing equipment whilst Steve brought items relating to the spiritual threat. They had even found time to call upon the local Roman Catholic Priest Father O'Callaghan on route. Nevertheless the wait had seemed like several hours to Liz who was close to breaking point. Liz welcomed them in with open arms, lots of hugs and lots of tears. Lauren, who was a very experienced Accident & Emergency nurse, immediately took Liz into the bedroom to look at her injuries and to make sure there hadn't actually been rape. She then gave Liz a complete check up including her vital signs; temperature, pulse and blood pressure and finally spent some time examining her hands and nails. Satisfied that physically they were only dealing with scratches on Liz's legs, Lauren cleaned her legs, wiped the wounds with antiseptic and put plasters on the worst cuts. The girls then came out the bedroom and joined Steve in the lounge.

Once they were all seated Steve looked at Lauren and asked what Liz's injuries consisted of. Lauren said "I am as sure as I can be, that we are dealing with a psychological attack Steve, not a physical one." Liz immediately screamed "But my legs are all scratched!" Lauren replied "I know, I treated them remember, but if you look at the scratches they are consistent with you scratching your legs, the scratches are all upwards and towards your groin. Also you have signs of skin under your nails." "Why the Hell would I do that?" Liz screamed. Steve replied "That is exactly what we need to find out." Steve turned and looked at Lauren "You are convinced of your findings Lauren?" "Yes" she said.

Steve said "Liz, firstly we need to look at what happened and why, and then address your absolute safety. Then finally we have to decide on how we remove the threat and ensure it will not happen again. Now I know and appreciate you are undergoing a massive trauma at present which will cause you a lot of mental stress, but I am not looking to address that as such. If we cure the problem the mental stress will go away. Does that make sense? Are you OK with that?" "Steve I am so pleased you two are here and feel with your help I have some chance of coping." "OK" Steve said, "let's get started. Do you have a close friend who will move in with you for a few days while we address these problems. This will not be solved in a day and you may not be able to cope at night on your own. You can't think about Sue because of the situation with Peter. You want someone who is unattached and preferably not working at present." "You know Cathy, Steve, I think she is still out of work and we get on very well" Liz replied. "OK" Steve said "give her a ring right now and explain that you are unwell and it's very serious. You must not start to tell her the truth over the phone. She must just accept it is serious and can she come and support you through it? Ask her if she would move in with you for a few days. If she says yes, get her to pack and come round now, so she is party to everything going on. That is essential. Ring her on your mainline in the bedroom, so you can talk more easily." "OK" Liz said and went off to the bedroom.

While Liz was on the phone Lauren went into the kitchen and made tea. She came back with a tray of tea and biscuits just as Liz came out of the bedroom. Liz gave a weak smile and said that Cathy was packing and will be over as soon as possible. While Lauren served tea Steve said to Liz he should explain what has happened so she will understand why he is doing certain things. "How is it you know what has happened, Steve?" Liz asked. Steve replied "Because I know what type of coven Peter has joined. Let me explain, it will take some time though. I will start with the Ouija board. This board was originally invented as a game but can nevertheless be used for medium-ship, divining and even prophesy by certain people. It's the people that make it work not the board itself. In my coven we also use water, mirrors, glass balls, tarot cards and tealeaves which can all be equally effective but again whatever the instrument it's the person or persons not the tool. However with the Ouija board there can be a definite attempt to get through to the other side. This means if the board is being seriously used for that, it should only ever be done inside a protective circle so you have some protection if you do attract something you don't like. You were therefore vulnerable Liz but you would never have realised how vulnerable. Do you remember asking me about Peter and I refused to put you in contact with him?" "Yes, I do, I couldn't understand why you were so awkward." "Well" Steve replied "were you aware Peter had joined a coven?" "Peter did say he had joined a coven and that it wasn't your coven. He also said you were not happy about it. I sort of assumed you were upset because he didn't come to you." "He did come to me" Steve replied but only to tell me he had joined this coven. I was very unhappy about it and told him to stop going to these people but I'm afraid he refused to take my advice. You see Liz that coven he is going to is a Satanic coven." "Oh my God!" Liz replied.

Steve stayed quiet for a few moments letting Liz take that in. Then he said "Peter must have broken a rule at one of their meetings and a demon has attached itself to him." "How do you know, Steve, that it's a demon?" "Because you told me it had called itself Daimon and Daimon is the Greek word for demon. The New Testament was originally written in Greek and on more than seventy occasions it refers to Daimons. When they translated the New Testament to English in King James's reign, they translated the Greek word Daimon into devil. Now, we would normally hope that if it's attached itself to Peter it has left your flat when he left but the fact that it seemed to visit you last night, would indicate it has possibly stayed. Moving out will not help, it's attracted to you not your flat. We have to fight this thing and drive it away. Its not here now or I would sense it, so we have to make sure it can't get back which is not straight forward." Liz then asked "But you said it was a psychological attack not a physical attack. It was a bad dream and it was me that made the scratches, so why are you so concerned to protect me?" Steve replied "Demons can't hurt you physically but they can attack your mind and that is exactly what it did. It gave you a terrible dream of it raping you so you became totally scared and scratched yourself. But it may not leave it at that. It will probably come back because demons usually want to stay. To stay it has to materialise and if it can't find a way it will enter you and use your body, you have heard of demonic possession I assume?" "Yes, certainly Steve, but I thought that was just in horror films." "Unfortunately not, Liz." Steve replied "If the demon gets inside you we are talking exorcism which must be avoided at all costs. We must keep it out of you by keeping it out of your flat." "How did it come into the flat then?" Liz worriedly asked.

Steve replied "An elemental, a spirit, a demon has to be invited into someone's home for the first time, to be able to get in. After that they can come and go as they like. This is our problem. If the demon was 'attached' to Peter he was invited in by inviting Peter in. As in the Bible when you invite someone into your house and you give him food and drink, that then seals the welcome. I guess you gave Peter food and drink. You don't have to say, but if you and Peter made love that would magnify the welcome ten fold. The greatest acts we humans can do is kill or give life. That is why all spiritual actions are magnified ten times if done with human sacrifice or sexual ritual. Few religions use human sacrifice now but sexual orgasm is the act of creating life and has the same effect, hence sexual rituals. You wouldn't have realised what you were doing or inviting."

Liz was still very scared but calmer now as she could at least see Steve understood the situation and she was trusting Steve to resolve it. "If you imagine" Steve continued "your flat is your castle and we have a monster outside. We have to pull up the drawbridge and not allow anyone in except the four of us plus Father O'Callaghan. If the milkman knocks we ignore it." "Why Father O'Callaghan Steve? He's a Roman Catholic Priest." "We are about to have a spiritual fight with the Dark side, the result of the evil of Satanism. We must not lose, we cannot lose. When this Country was fighting the Nazis in the second world war we fought alongside the French and Americans. Not all of the British like both of these nations but they had similar beliefs to us and the same goals. Roman Catholics have very similar beliefs and goals to us Pagans, they were Pagans once. They believe in respect for life, caring for their fellow man, conservation of our planet, protecting all nature, and love and forgiveness not lust and hate. Most of the Roman Catholic ceremonies are based upon their previous Pagan ancestry. We are brothers without arms, at least not guns. We are fighting for the Light to win over the Dark. Father O'Callaghan has asked for my assistance in the past and will give us what we need this time. He can supply the 'host' which because of two thousand years of belief is still one of the greatest weapons to protect us from the Darkness. Also whether you call her the Goddess or the Mother of God, she will protect us from this evil from Hell." Liz then said "I wish I had known half of this before, this is a very hard way to learn." At that moment there was a ring from the front door bell. "Leave the door and phone calls to me" Steve said "I'll go."

Steve came back into the lounge with Cathy who was carrying a suitcase and looked very worried. He turned and looked at Cathy. "Please Cathy I know you are very worried but give me two minutes to organise Liz, and then I'll explain everything to you. Put your suitcase in the bedroom and then make yourself comfortable over there" Steve said, pointing at one of the comfy chairs. Cathy nodded. Then Steve said to Liz "We must now start preparing as quickly as possible. It is already nearly 11am, what time does it get dark now? About 4pm? That gives us only 5 hours of daylight to prepare. Right Liz you have to assume you and Cathy are locked in your flat for 5 days, it shouldn't be that long but better to be safe than sorry. Sit down with paper and pen and start writing a shopping list for the two of you. Food and drink are a problem though. Whilst this spiritual struggle continues none of us can eat meat or drink alcohol. You need to restrict yourselves to fruit, vegetables, dairy products, bread and soft drinks. Otherwise the list must include everything else you will need, toiletries, personal needs, medication, and magazines. Make sure we have enough soap and face clothes for 4 people showering everyday and sometimes twice a day. Remember that until this is resolved neither of you are going anywhere. Give the list to Lauren and either the money or your bank card and pin code. This is not the time to distrust her. You can change the pin code again when this is all over."

Now while Liz looked for paper and pen and started her shopping list, Steve sat Cathy down and explained that Liz was not physically ill but in great danger nevertheless. He told her about Peter, the Satanic coven Peter had just joined, the Ouija board, the appearance of this demon and what happened last night to Liz. Cathy was visibly moved and obviously wanted to go and hug Liz but she could see Liz was busy and she had heard what Steve had said about the time being short. When Liz finished her shopping list Steve told her to give it to Cathy so she could check if there was anything else she would need and then, when they were both satisfied the list was complete, to give the list plus her card and pin number to Lauren. "But don't leave quite yet Lauren" Steve instructed. Cathy had moved next to Liz on the sofa as it was easier to go through the shopping list with her there. Steve then turned to Liz and Cathy and said "Then the two of you must make a list of everyone to ring and ring them explaining you will be away or unwell or whatever you like for the next week. Liz you must book off sick at work for a week which in your case means cancelling all photo shoots and both of you must cancel any appointments for anything at all in the next week. Just remember the doors will be locked and the phones disconnected, all of them, mobile phones as well. Your iPhones, iPads, lap tops, computers, game consoles, televisions and radios will be unplugged. There must be no conduit that the monster can use." At that Steve jumped up and went round the flat counting. When he had finished Liz asked him what he was counting. "The openings, external doors and windows. These will have to be defended. There are six."

Steve turned and looked at Lauren, "Please grab your pad and pen Lauren." When she had, Steve continued "When Liz gives you her list, please add on two dozen tall white candles and seven candle sticks. Make sure the candles fit the candlesticks and the candlesticks are sturdy and stable, they mustn't fall over easily. Five hand torches and enough batteries for at least one set of spares for every torch. Bottles of still water for four people for five days, the number of bottles depends on the size of the bottles of course plus a few extra to make Holy water. Also a dozen large salt containers, the type that have a spout and you can pour, six besom brooms, seven small bowls like the finger bowls used on a table and in case there are accidents a plastic bucket with a lid if possible and a large packet of wet wipes. Finally get necklaces for Liz and Cathy. Get two with Pagan pentagrams and two with Christian crosses, the bigger the better." Liz heard this and looked up from making her list of people to ring and said "How do these crosses or pentagrams work Steve?" "It's like this Liz" Steve replied "Many of the Police Forces in the world use a star or even a pentagram as their badge and on their warrant cards. When the police officer holds that warrant card out it has the power to protect him or enforce the law. The star has no real power in fact, it is powerful because the policeman believes in it and so do we. When the Roman Catholic Priest holds out a cross or I hold out a pentagram it works because we believe in it."

At that moment the front door bell chimed and Steve went to answer it. It was Father O'Callaghan and he followed Steve back into the lounge carrying what looked like a doctor's bag. "Father" Steve said "You have met Lauren before haven't you, as you know she is my High Priestess and my right hand man in all things spiritual." Father O'Callaghan held out his hand to Lauren and shook her hand with genuine warmth. "Father this is Liz who is our damsel in distress and Cathy her wonderful friend at a time of need." The Father then said "It's lovely to meet you ladies but I wish it was in better circumstances." At that point Lauren jumped up and said "Sorry Father I have to go." She looked at Steve and said "I have the completed list and card, can I use your car Steve, there is a lot of stuff on this list?" "Of course" and Steve threw her his keys "tell me when you get back and I'll help you bring it all up to the flat." Lauren said "OK" as she hurried out the flat.

Steve sat down with Father O'Callaghan and proceeded to bring the Father up to date, although nothing much had altered from what Steve had told him earlier. Father produced a black box the size of a large chocolate box and opened it. From the box Father took out another small box and eight small bottles. "Here we have eight 'hosts' and eight bottles of 'holy water' as requested. They have all been blessed at the altar, by myself. Please return whatever you can, I can't bare to think that hosts or holy water are left lying around. Also should the Church find out, for me to remain a Priest I would have to join your coven. The Holy Roman Catholic Church would dispense with my services. The Holy Water would be a point of concern but the missing 'hosts' would carry the death penalty. Well, very nearly anyway." Steve was very moved, he put his arms around Father O'Callaghan and gave him a big hug. Liz was watching this and felt it had probably been a long time since anyone had hugged Father like that. Steve knew only too well the risk Father was taking and the trust he was putting in Steve. Steve put the eight bottles of Holy water and the small box of hosts into his own bag for safety.

"As you know Father" Steve said "all the phones whether mainline or mobile will be switched off before nightfall today but I have your mobile number Father, and I will ring you or call-in to tell you how it is going and invite you to join us if you wish." Father O'Callaghan stood up, smiled at Steve and said "Steve, you and your friends, may God bless you and keep you safe." He then drew a cross in the air and said "In Nomine Patris et Filii et Spiritus Sancti"(Latin for: In the name of the Father, and the Son and the Holy Spirit) he walked back to the front door and let himself out. After Father O'Callaghan left Liz looked at Steve and asked "Can I ask Steve what is in that little black box? I think I heard you both refer to it as 'hosts'? I get the impression it is very special."

"It is 'they' not 'it' Liz, as there are several, eight in fact, but you are right Liz they are very very special. I know you are not a practicing Christian but I'm sure you are familiar with altar bread also known as communion bread or the Eucharist. During the communion the Priest offers you bread in memory of 'the body of Christ' and then wine in the memory of 'the blood of Christ'. In many Christian churches the altar bread has a very special and Holy significance. The Roman Catholics used to believe that the altar bread changed into the body of Christ when it was blessed by the Priest. They called it 'transubstantiation'. After the Priest's blessing the altar bread, as it was now the actual 'body of Christ,' then became known as the 'host'. This comes from the Latin word 'hostia' which means sacrificial victim, which of course refers to Jesus himself being sacrificed to save our sins. Most Roman Catholics and Roman Catholic Priests that I have spoken to recently now accept that the bread and wine represent the body and blood of Jesus and do not actually transubstantiate.

Nevertheless the significance of the host is astounding. Many Catholic churches insist the host is only made out of four ingredients, wheat, water, yeast and salt and some insist the water used must be Holy water. They also sometimes restrict those doing the baking to Christians only and sometimes they must have confession beforehand. The 'host' signifies the hopes and beliefs of millions of worshippers around the world and therefore commands a huge spiritual power in itself. The greatest physical weapon in this world against evil is without doubt the host. Watch the way the Priest gives the host at communion and how a silver salver is held below the communicant's chin to catch the slightest crumb that falls." "Thank you Steve," Liz said "the communion wafers have taken on a whole new meaning to me."

In the meantime Liz and Cathy had gone into the bedroom and were making phone calls and Steve decided to go and make some more tea. He couldn't remember whether Liz and Cathy had milk and sugar so put a small sugar bowl and milk jug on the tray. When he returned to the lounge Liz and Cathy were back sitting together on the sofa speaking in low conspiratorial whispers. "Help yourself to your tea Liz." She smiled and did so. Cathy followed suit. "Earlier I explained our situation as a castle with a monster outside." Steve said "That is a fairly good image excepting at the moment we don't have any defences, no moat, no portcullises, no heavily barred gates. So that is what we have to build, defences. We need to build two lines of defence, an outer wall and an inner wall. We might as well relax with our tea at present because we need the supplies that Lauren is getting. While we wait I will go through the basic plan. Liz, you I'm afraid, will be on house arrest for as long as this takes. We cannot take any chances for all the reasons I said earlier. Cathy you really need to stay with Liz at all times, especially after dark. Lauren and I will come and go depending on the situation. It may well mean we have to stay all night with you both but we will play it by ear. I suggest you both think of all your friends and family and any work colleagues and make sure you have rung everyone you have to. We really don't want some desperate relative or friend telling the police you have gone missing. A police raid in the middle of this would be a disaster. Can you imagine explaining to the police what is happening here. If you think of anyone you should have rung please do so immediately as you won't be able to later."

The front door bell chimed and Steve got up and went to the door. It was Lauren and she had managed to park right outside. They set up a chain with Liz in the kitchen to put things away, Cathy running between the front door and kitchen, Steve on the stairs bringing the goods up to the front door and Lauren unloading. The car was unloaded in ten minutes and Liz and Cathy decided to make some lunch for everyone, pilchards on toast and tea. With no meat their choices were going to become repetitive.

By the time they had finished lunch it was nearly 2pm and Steve and Lauren wanted to start preparations for the night but before that, while the phones were still working, Steve needed to ring Peter. He went into the bedroom and dialled Peter's number. It was Friday but being Boxing day Steve hoped the café was closed and Peter would be home. He was not disappointed, Peter answered on the third ring. Peter was very surprised to hear from Steve. Steve said he had something very serious to discuss and has Peter got a few minutes to talk. He said he had. "Peter we have a major problem" and then went on to describe the story Liz had told him about the Ouija board and the black shadow. He told Peter how it named itself as a Demon and then what happened later in the night including the scratches Liz received on her legs. Without doubt Peter was very distressed. He said he had had a wonderful day with Liz up to that point and had really hoped that they would have a relationship. "Steve, I had no idea what had happened and was completely confused when Liz threw me out of her flat very suddenly on Christmas evening. Do you think this thing came from the Satanic circle? Could it have just arrived because of the Ouija board?" Peter asked.

"Well the truth is I don't know" Steve said "but it would be a big coincidence if this Demon happened to turn up just after you join a Satanic coven. Peter you need to understand that Liz is close to a mental breakdown, she is very scared and I really do hate to say this but all her friends and my coven members blame you for what has happened. I told you it was dangerous to mix with these people, you ignored my warnings and Liz is paying the penalty. I am very afraid Liz is at risk of demonic possession. You need to go to the Satanic High Priest immediately and tell him what has happened. No-one has done this deliberately. You need to ask him if there is anything he can do to send this Demon back to Hell. It is just possible he may be able to explain to you what has happened and resolve it. I have no idea what ceremonies or workings they do, so he will be in a better position to establish what has happened. He may also be able to discover whether the Demon is still attached to you and if so he may be able to identify it and send it back. In the meantime I am putting Liz in a protective circle. If possible I will ring you later tonight to see how you got on with the Satanic High Priest. I will ring you on your home number. If I can't get you on that, what is your mobile number?" Peter told Steve his mobile number and promised he would go round to the Satanic coven's High Priest right now. Steve replied "If I don't ring you it's because I have had to join Liz in the circle and it's too risky to leave her. In that case I'll ring you as soon as I can."

Steve returned to the lounge and told everyone what he had said to Peter. "We cannot assume anything may come of that, so we have to prepare for the worst. Now I explained earlier how you can think of this place as our castle and we have a monster outside. However you have to remember this fight is not physical, it is spiritual. Think of it as a psychological struggle, but one we daren't lose. We have to close any incoming or outgoing channels such as radio, television, broadband and telephones, which a Demon may be able to make use of. We have to seal all entrances and exits against spiritual attack, however doors and windows will also be locked. If our spiritual defences don't work the locks are useless against this creature. He will just walk through walls, a locked door is a waste of time against him. However every door and window still needs to be locked because we do not want any human walking in and accidently breaking into our circle. So these preparations are spiritual defences but also physical defences to stop a misguided human's interference. That is why earlier on, you telephoned everyone you know so they wouldn't come round looking for you. Now we build our castle defences."

CHAPTER 8

The Protective Circle

They started off their preparations by clearing all the furniture out of the lounge into the second bedroom. Then each of them took a besom broom and carefully swept the floor. When Steve was satisfied he took five of the brooms, and taking one broom at a time blessed it in the name of Eostra the Goddess and laid it across a window. After doing this to both of the bedroom windows, the kitchen window, the bathroom window and the lounge window he had only one broom left which would be for the front door. He then took one of the salt containers held it high, dedicated it to Eostra, and said "blessings be in the name of Eostra, upon this creature of salt." He again walked to each window sprinkling salt across the base of the windows and each time called upon Eostra to protect and seal these openings. He placed the salt container and last broom by the front door ready to seal that door when the time came. He then warned Liz and Cathy against disturbing the brooms or salt.

He took Lauren, Liz and Cathy into the kitchen and whilst he made tea for them he explained about clothing. "Ideally we should all shower and then prepare the circle skyclad but as you Liz and Cathy are not coven members you will find that very strange and embarrassing, we will have to find clean clothes instead." "What is skyclad" Cathy asked. "Being only dressed by the sky, naked in other words" "Oh Hell" Cathy said. "You are best advised not to use the word 'Hell' from now on for any reason and also not to blaspheme in any way. The point Cathy is that we are about to create a sacred space in this lounge and nothing dirty or contaminated must be in that circle. That includes us. We can get around it, as we do in the coven on cold winter nights," Lauren smiled at Steve at that point. "We put on ceremonial robes which are carefully washed and never worn outside the circle. Liz and Cathy will have to use suitable clean clothing instead. Right you two (looking at Liz and Cathy again) must find nightdresses or pyjamas that are just washed and are absolutely totally clean. Do not wear anything else on your feet or in the way of underclothes unless you absolutely have to. Remember strictly you are supposed to be skyclad.

Lauren and I will leave you for a little while return to our homes and shower and return with our gowns." Liz immediately panicked and said "But you can't leave us alone Steve!" "Its fine Liz, you will be safe in the daytime as long as you do not sleep. Cathy, just make sure Liz does not 'nod off' even for a second. Even when Liz goes to the bathroom to shower or use the toilet you must stay with her. Her sanity and possibly her life depend upon it. Do you understand?" "Yes Steve, I will look after her." "Right" Steve said "We'll be back very soon. I need to take your front door key." Liz went and got it for him. "Liz and Cathy, do not answer the phone or the door under any circumstances. Whoever is standing there calling probably won't be who you think it is, do you both understand what I am saying?" They both nodded. "Say yes," Steve said. They did. "When washed and dressed in your clean clothes sit here on the floor and wait for us. As I said ignore any shouts, knocks on the door or phone calls." Steve and Lauren went to the front door and let themselves out, locking it behind them.

Liz and Cathy looked through their newly washed clothes and both chose pyjamas which had loose tops and leggings and were clean and unworn. They both then went into the bathroom and stayed together in there, whilst each of them showered. When they came out dressed in their pyjamas they sat quietly on what was now a clean floor.

Steve drove to Lauren's house and waited while she showered and collected a few more items including her ceremonial gown. She dressed in clean clothes for the journey and then they went onto Steve's house where he also showered, redressed and picked up his clean ceremonial gown. It was under an hour later when they returned to Liz's flat and Liz and Cathy's relief was very evident when they walked in. "Well" said Lauren "did you get any knocks on the door or phone calls?" "No, not a thing" Liz said. Steve replied "Didn't expect anything before night fall but had to say what I did, in case. OK got a lot to do let's get busy," and Steve collected his bag and took out a box of writing chalk, a ball of string and sissors, and a compass.

With Steve and Lauren directing preparations they formed a protective circle. This involved Liz standing in the middle of the room holding a long piece of string tightly to the ground whilst Lauren tied a chalk to the other end and then drew a circle on the floor. Lauren then increased the length of the string by a foot and drew a second circle round the outside of the first. Steve laid the compass on the ground to check where North was and made a small mark on the inner circle. Steve then knelt on the ground in front of that chalk mark and very slowly and meticulously wrote in large bold letters between the two circle lines working clockwise around the circle, the following words: **In nomine Patris et Filii et Spiritus Sancti Michael Gabriel Raphael Uriel Thronus Dominationes principalis virtutes Cherubim et Seraphim.** Steve must have done this many times to not only know these words by heart but was able to space them so that they completed the circle and were equidistant. "Can I please ask you Steve" Liz said "what you have written there." "The first eight words" Steve replied "are in Latin and mean, in the name of the Father and Son and Holy Spirit. The remaining words are the names of the Holy Angels and Arch Angels." "How would you know their names Steve?" Cathy asked.

"Well I am sure you have heard of Moses in the Bible. It is written that God revealed seven books to his faithful servant Moses on Mount Sinai, two of which were books of Magick and gave Moses the powers he needed to form his nation and control his people. These two books were passed to Aaron, Caleb, Joshua, David, his son Solomon and his High Priest Sadock. They were referred to as Biblis Arcanum Arcanorum, which means Mystery of all Mysteries. However they were hidden from David by Solomon's High Priest Sadock but were discovered in 330 AD by the first Christian Roman Emperor Constantine the Great and were sent to Pope Sylvester in Rome. They were naturally referred to as The Sixth and Seventh Books of Moses. The books show the Seals of the Angels of Power and of the Seven Planets and spirits and The Seal of the Ministering Throne Angels and the True Seal of the choir of Hosts or Dominations of the Ministering Angels. The books of Moses set out spells or conjurations as they are called to achieve power. The names of the Holy Angels and Arch Angels together with many other Angels are listed in these books." "How is it you know these names, even if they are written in these books?" Liz asked. Steve replied "These books were translated from Hebrew to Latin and later into English with the exception of the actual seals of magic which have had to remain in Hebrew and I have a copy of both books." This revelation was received in a stunned silence.

"We must get on" Steve said, and with that proceeded to draw the five pointed star of the Pagan pentagram, the tips of the star touching the outer circle. Again, the star was so well drawn it was obvious Steve had done this many times. Whilst he did this Lauren was setting a white candle in a candlestick at the tip of each of the five points of the star and then proceeded to put a small bowl in each of the five valleys of the star and a little water in each bowl. Steve was following Lauren around the circle and was putting a little dried mandrake root by the candle and then holding each bowl up and blessing it 'exorcising this creature of water in the name of the Goddess Eostra.' By now it was approaching 3.30 pm so they were running out of daytime. Steve told Liz and Cathy to get as many sheets and blankets that they could that were washed and unused and pile them in the centre of the circle but they must tread very carefully over the chalk lines and Angels names. If the circle was smudged it would destroy the circle's protection. They were then to collect the dressing table's stool which had a hard top and would be perfect for a makeshift altar. After they had placed the stool in the circle they were to put all the bottles of water in the circle plus a supply of fruit. In the meantime Lauren and Steve put the batteries in the five torches and checked they worked. They then placed Steve's bag, the four necklaces with the crosses and pentagrams, the torches, spare batteries, all the boxes of matches and the plastic bucket and the big box of wet wipes, in the circle. Steve then picked up one of Father O'Callaghan's little bottles from his bag and went to the front door and made sure it was locked and bolted. He placed the besom broom across the entrance, sprinkled 'Holy Water' from the bottle around the door frame and said loudly 'In Nomine Patris et Filii et Spiritus Sancti' because this Holy Water had been blessed by Father O'Callaghan. He

ıll five windows were all locked tight and again sprinkled
ınd the frames and blessed them in Latin.

..ıs was all done he returned to the circle and carefully
ʀʀıng over the chalk lines he said to the three ladies "My dear
friends I now come to the embarrassing bit. Liz and Cathy, you guys
cannot leave this circle during the hours of darkness whatever may
happen. That means you should now consider using the toilet. The
problem is if you are frightened in the night you can't go back there so
we all have to accept that. In an emergency Lauren or I could consider
leaving the circle as we are practiced in protecting ourselves but it is
not safe for you to do so. You two must not under any circumstances
leave the circle whatever happens. I suggest the two of you (looking
at Liz and Cathy) return to the bathroom for a while. You must
however stay together as I said earlier. Do not leave each-other even
for a second." Whilst Liz and Cathy were in the bathroom Lauren and
Steve opened out the sheets and blankets and made the centre of the
circle as comfortable as possible. They put their supplies in one tidy
pile to keep as much room as possible for the four of them. Steve then
left the circle and walked around the flat disconnecting everything,
the phones, the television, the radio. the computer, and the incoming
broadband line. Everything was switched off and unplugged. He then
went to the central heating controller and turned it to 24 hours and
set the temperature to 21 degrees. Then he walked around the flat
again and turned on every light in every room. By now Liz and Cathy
had returned and Lauren had gone into the bathroom. Once Lauren
returned Steve also went in the bathroom. As Steve returned he looked
through the lounge window and noticed it was beginning to get dark
outside. Steve looked at the three ladies and said "If you haven't already
done so turn your mobile phones off, and I don't mean onto silent, I
mean switch it off and leave it outside the circle." Steve and Lauren
then went to the bedroom and collected their ceremonial gowns and
walked towards the circle. They both unselfconsciously stripped off
their clothes so that they were completely naked. They pulled their
gowns over their heads and stepped into the circle.

Everyone settled in the centre of the circle and made themselves
as comfortable as possible. Steve then said "We need to discuss what
may happen. It is quite possible nothing may happen and all this has

been unnecessary. However if this Demon does come back it will be to attack Liz, so we need to understand how we can protect her and of course ourselves as well. The Demon has no way of materialising unless it is able to take possession of someone's body, which we will not allow, so the attack will not be physical. The Demon will not be able to get into the flat because of our defences so it will use its ability to affect our minds. It will do one of two things or possibly both. It will put ideas into your head, like I have been telling you rubbish and it's safe to leave the circle and open the front door. Or it will pretend to be a friend or member of your family who is pleading to come into the flat. It can sound like them and sometimes even look like them by putting their image into your head. You may even see someone you know and trust standing outside the circle, a Demon can do that. Doubt everything you see and hear, stay together and stay in the circle and you will be safe. Each of us must keep a close eye on each-other and shout out if we realise one of us is under attack. Now I must set up an altar and seal this circle of protection."

Steve took the four necklaces and gave Liz and Cathy one each with a cross and one each with a pentagram, with the request to put them on and not remove them for any reason. He then reached over and took the dressing table stool and took it to the edge of the circle where he had marked it with the chalk signifying it was the North. He then took his bag and removed a black cloth with a large gold pentagram on it. He placed it over the altar so that a single point of the pentagram was upwards. He then took out of his bag a gold plated pentagram mounted on a plinth and set it in the centre of the altar. He took the two remaining candle sticks, put candles in them and placed them on the altar. Then he took the two remaining small bowls and set them on the altar. He put water in one bowl and salt in the other. With great care and respect he took out the small black box the Father had given him with the hosts inside and the remaining seven bottles of Holy water and placed them all on the altar. Lastly he took a large ornate knife (an Athame) from his bag and laid it next to the box. He was ready to seal the circle. Starting at the East he called upon the Guardians of the Watchtower and the spirits for the East representing Air and blessed the Gods and asked for their protection as he lit the candle. He moved clockwise around the circle repeating this until all the candles were alight. He then went back to the East raised the small bowl of water and dedicated it to the Gods of Light and blessed it and then walked around the circle sprinkling the Holy water on the edge of the circle. He then did the same with the salt making sure there was salt all the way round the edge. Twice he had to top up the bowl and bless it again before continuing. Then he took the box of hosts and very carefully took one out at a time and placed it between the lines of the two circles where the pentagram points crossed the lines crying "In Nomine Patris et Filii et Spiritus Sancti." Finally he stood in the centre of the circle holding the Athame pointing it to the candle of the East, he was summoning up all the energies from the ground through his feet, up his legs, up his body, down his arm, into his hand and into the Athame so that the power transmitted where he was pointing at the edge of the circle, as he rotated clockwise, laying a barrier of protection. As he did so he called out loudly:

> "As the Mystery of the second seal, from the Sixth Book of Moses, I call upon and conjure thee, Spirit Phuel, by the Holy messengers and all the disciples of the Lord, by the four Holy Evangelists and the three Holy Men of God and by the most terrible and most Holy words Abriel, Fibriel, Zada, Zaday, Zarabo, Laragola, Lavaterium, Laroyol, Zay, Zagin, Labir, Lya, Adeo, Deus, Alon, Abay, Alos, Pieus, Ehos, Mihi, Uini, Mora, and Zorad. By all things Holy. By all the Gods, Angels and Arch Angels of Light. We ask for protection in this circle against everything evil and against the Power of Darkness."

Steve then looked at his three colleagues and said "Because of the seriousness of the threat to Liz, to ensure her protection, I have invoked The Mystery of the Second Seal from The Sixth Book of Moses. As two of us are not initiated coven members you have to confirm your faith in each-other and the circle. I will do the act of faith with the High Priestess and then Liz and then Cathy. You two need to copy what Lauren does and says. Steve turned towards Lauren and held the Athame point against her throat and then he loudly said "It is better that you rush upon this blade than enter this circle with fear in your heart. How do you enter?" Lauren replied loudly "I enter the circle with total love and total trust." Steve smiled and lowered the Athame and they then kissed each-other on a cheek. Steve then repeated the act of faith with Liz and then Cathy. Steve then held the Athame up towards the sky and shouted "As above" and then pointed the Athame downwards at the Earth and shouted "so below. This circle is sealed. So mote it be." Steve then said "Each of you must now take a Bible and look up Psalm 23 and leave the Bible open at that page. If you start to get thoughts that are not your own, tell the others and start reading out loud psalm 23 over and over again to block out these thoughts. However you must relax now while you can, it may be a very long night. If the Demon does come we will be warned of its presence as the temperature will drop and the lights may flicker or even go out."

In the meantime Peter had decided to drive around to Aleister's house and ask for his help. The great entrance gates opened as he drove up to them as though he was expected. He parked in front of the house as usual and walked up the steps to the large entrance doors. They too started to open before he even reached them, welcoming but very scary as though they were waiting for him. Castor was there in the entrance hall and nodded at him and turned towards the lounge doors. Peter followed Castor into the lounge and found Dame Alice and Aleister standing there waiting for him. "I understand you have an unwelcome visitor Peter" Aleister said. Peter was about to say how the hell did you know that and then remembered who he was speaking to. Of course he would know what was going on. 'Whatever happens in the future' Peter thought 'I mustn't make an enemy of this man.' "Yes High Priest, I was playing on an Ouija board with a friend and she saw a black shadow behind me. By using the Ouija board it named itself as Daimon. But it didn't stop there. Later that night, my friend had a terrifying dream of being raped by this Demon and woke up in the morning with deep scratches on her legs. Can you tell me if this Demon is attached to me and if so how I get rid of it?" "Normally Peter if I have an issue with a Demon I will invoke it and then banish it. But we have a problem. I have no idea what Demon this is, so I can't invoke it. I can call the coven together for tomorrow evening and we will look and see if you have a familiar or Demon with you. If you haven't, I would then have to go to the place it was last seen, your friend Liz's flat at Reginald Crescent in Newhaven and summon it, but I don't think your friend Steve would want that." Peter looked as white as a sheet, he realised then, that Aleister could see every move he made. Where he went, who he was with and everything that he did! Peter then stammered his reply "Can I ask you..... High Priest...... to try the first option.........to call the coven together..... for tomorrow.......... ... Saturday night, ...please." "Peter, be here at 10pm. Just bring your domino, clean of course. I will see you then." "That's perfect" Peter said "I am working tomorrow but will be home by 8pm." Peter then realised Castor had entered the lounge and was standing behind him, waiting for him. Peter turned and followed Castor to the front doors. As Peter left, Aleister asked Alice to come in tomorrow, Saturday, at 9pm, and to phone four of their members to come as well. "They are needed to call the corners so we can form a circle. But make sure they are experienced members Alice, it's just possible we will be confronting a Demon".

Peter drove home very thoughtful. When he got home he tried several times to ring Steve but there was no answer from Steve's mainline phone and his mobile was either disconnected or switched off. He really hoped he could help solve this problem and that Liz would forgive him if he did. He went to bed and slept fitfully.

CHAPTER 9

The Demon Returns

Outside it was getting dark, but in Liz's lounge it was warm and very bright. The central heating was on and every light in the flat shone brightly. Steve, Lauren, Liz and Cathy only had minimal clothes on but they were if anything, too warm. Steve told them to each choose one of the four candles and then sit down with their feet towards that candle. They then wriggled about until they had their backs comfortably against each-other. "You might be sitting like this all night without anything happening so make sure you are as comfortable as possible" Lauren said. They moved the sheets and blankets about a bit and wriggled a bit more until they were fairly settled. Lauren then said "As Steve says, make sure you don't damage the chalk lines and whatever happens stay as you are now." Steve had his head bowed and eyes shut and from appearances could have been asleep. The others followed his example.

It was now dark outside, a wind had got up and it had started to rain. Each of them listened to the wind blowing around the flat and the rain on the lounge window pane. Nothing at all happened and by midnight Liz and Cathy were beginning to wonder if they were not all mad and could be comfortably in their own beds. After a little while longer Cathy said to Steve "Are you sure this is necessary Steve? Wouldn't we be just as safe in our own beds and much more comfortable?" Steve immediately raised his head and said "It is starting. The Demon is putting thoughts of doubt in your heads, he wants you to doubt me, he wants you to ignore my instructions and he will try to convince you to leave the circle and open a window or the front door. You must ignore these thoughts. Now hold hands and don't let go whatever happens. That way we protect each-other." The time ticked by, nothing happening.

Then they all noticed a strange small sound. It sounded like a mouse gnawing at one of the skirting boards. It was a very small sound and not threatening in any way but yet it was. The sound seemed to invade the circle. They could no longer hear the wind or the rain on the window pane, just this scratch, scratch, gnaw, gnawing sound of an imaginary mouse. Then they noticed it had definitely got colder. Steve said "We need to start chanting Psalm 23, the first four verses, as you all need to know it by heart for when the lights go out, in case the candles also go out." They all grabbed their Bibles and put them on their laps, re-clasped each-other's hands and started reading "The Lord is my shepherd, I shall not want. He maketh me to lie down in green pastures, He leadeth me besides the still waters, He restoreth my soul. He guides me in paths of righteousness for His name's sake. Even though I walk through the valley of the shadow of death, I will fear no evil, for though art with me, Thy rod and Thy staff they comfort me." As they were saying these verses for the third time the coldness intensified and the lights started getting dimmer.

*** The Grimorium Verum shows
the full Sigil of Lucifer as:

Steve told them all to stand up, staying in their circle with their backs to each-other. "Continue to hold each-other's hands and put your feet so they touch each-other. My left foot touches Liz's right foot. Liz's left foot touches Cathy's right. You get the idea." Liz suddenly said "I'm beginning to shiver and I can see my breath. It's getting really cold." As she said that, the lights all flickered and a draft of cold wind blew across the circle. At the same moment there was a knock on the door. Liz and Cathy looked at each-other then Steve, with panic in their eyes. "Don't panic, don't worry" Steve said "I'll do the talking if it's necessary." At that, a voice said in a lovely Irish brogue "I've come back to help you all, it's Father O'Callaghan." Liz immediately started to panic "How are we to let him in? We can't ignore him when he is trying to help us." "You must stay quiet Liz. I said I'll do the talking" Steve replied "that is not the Father. He knows we'll be in a circle and couldn't dare break it." Steve looked towards the front door and shouted "Go away you are not welcome here." It replied "I AM Father O'Callaghan." "Then tell me loud and strong that you worship Mary the mother of God and Jesus the son of God." "Aaaaah!!" was a strangled cry that sounded like whatever it was had just touched the hot plate.

It then went quiet but it was an unnatural quiet, a brooding tense feeling. It was what submariners felt when down below waiting for depth charges. Each of them found themselves holding their breaths, waiting for the explosion. Lauren said "Pull your necklaces out of your pyjamas so the crosses and pentagrams are clearly to be seen." As she was saying that, they all noticed that there were shadows were there weren't before and the shadows were slowly lengthening. It was still deathly quiet. No sound inside the lounge and no sound outside the window, not even a distant gull squawking in the wind, as they do. A very unnatural silence, pregnant with fear and trepidation, dominated the room. Steve said to start saying the 23rd Psalm again and started them off "The Lord is my shepherd, I shall not want. He maketh me to lie down in green pastures, He leadeth me besides the still waters, He restoreth my soul. He guides me in paths of righteousness for His name's sake. Even though I walk through the valley of the shadow of death, I will fear no evil, for though art with me, Thy rod and Thy staff they comfort me." Although now from memory, they were doing well and they got better and stronger each time they said it. The 23rd Psalm has a magickal quality and they were able to lose themselves in the saying of it, removing some of the fear that radiated the room. Steve encouraged them to keep going and speak louder and louder and stronger. "The thing outside can't hurt you physically as long as you don't move out the circle and it will struggle to hurt your mind if you keep focused on the Psalm and remember everything you hear and see is false. It is projected into your head. It's not real."

The wind in the room had now returned but was weak at first. However slowly it was getting stronger and stronger. The lights continued to get dimmer until there was but a mere glow in the light bulbs and the room was virtually in darkness except for the candles. The flames of the candles were being buffeted by the wind which now blew around the circle as though they were sitting in the vortex of a small hurricane. Then Liz cried out "Look into the corner over there!" pointing into the corner nearest the entrance door to the lounge. "Don't let go of each-other's hands, not for a moment!" shouted Steve, and Liz and Cathy immediately grabbed each-other's hands again. But they were all now staring into that corner as the shadow was definitely deeper and seemed to be forming a dark shape. The shape was solidifying into a broad but low creature. Two bright red dots were appearing and seemed to be eyes, under which was a snout and a mouth full of canine teeth that dripped saliva. Steve began to realise it was an image of a wolf, a hound from Hell. "Stay perfectly still" Steve said. "It is only an image in our heads. If it was real it wouldn't have been able to get into this room. The Demon is trying to panic us into breaking out of the circle. Then you would be in serious trouble."

Steve brought his two hands together so that Liz and Lauren's hands touched and told them to let go of his hands and to grasp each-other. He picked up one of the torches and turned it on and then went over to the altar and took two of Father O'Callaghan's bottles of Holy Water. Steve went very carefully to the edge of the East side of the circle, using the torch as it was now very dark. Apart from his torch only the flickering candles provided light, and he had to ensure he did not damage the protective circle. As he stood on the edge of the circle he had to shout to the others to be heard over the circling wind. "Do not move an inch, this thing may leap up at me and you mustn't jump back as it may damage the circle" Steve shouted. "Like I said, stay very still and keep holding each-others hands." He had hardly got these words out when the hound reared up on its hind legs. It was a mere six feet away from Steve and towered over him, standing over seven feet on its hind legs. Its eyes were red and its mouth was wide open showing a set of huge yellow canine teeth from which saliva continued to drip. Its breath smelled of rotten meat. It was everything that an evil mind would imagine to conjure up that would frighten most people to death, but Steve knew it couldn't be real, or at least he hoped it wasn't. As the saying goes he was betting his life on it. Probably betting his soul as well. Suddenly it leaped at Steve but crashed into an invisible wall at the edge of the circle and fell back. Liz and Cathy had cried out in fear but they had held their ground and hadn't fallen back. As the hound picked itself up and readied itself to leap again Steve took the top off the bottle of Holy water and shouted at the hound "In nomine Patris et Filii et Spiritus Sancti" as he threw the Holy water at the creature. There was a terrible scream, like a human scream, a flash of light, smoke and a smell of burning.

The wind had immediately stopped and as the smoke cleared and the burning smell dissipated, the lights became brighter and silence returned. This time however it was a different type of silence. The atmosphere of fear and dread had gone and the four of them looked at each-other for reassurance that they were all ok. When they realised they were all unharmed they threw their arms around each-other and Liz wept. They looked then at Steve for guidance who said "We are fine but I don't actually know about the Demon. I don't think that hound creature was real. I don't think it was the Demon itself. The Demon wouldn't have been able to get into this room due to the spiritual barriers we placed at the door and windows, which means the Demon must have projected that hound into our minds. As I said earlier you cannot believe anything you see or hear when dealing with a Demon." "If that is the case Steve, then that hound could not have hurt us, just scared us" said Liz.

"Unfortunately that is not true Liz. It may not be safe for us to leave the circle until morning, so I suggest we make ourselves comfortable on the sheets, blankets and pillows and I'll answer your question" said Steve as he proceeded to make himself comfortable. Once they were all seated and settled Steve explained, "I totally understand your thinking Liz but I need to tell you a story. It's a true story of when I was at University studying psychology. We were reading about the mind and its control on all the areas of the body and a few of us were playing with experiments relating to how the body responded when the mind was totally convinced of something which was in fact not true. We came up with this crazy test.

We found an unused room away from normal activity. Using heavy mettle brackets we fixed a chair to the wooden floor in front of an open fire grate. We put straps around the arms and the front legs of the chair. We made up a coal fire and left the poker stuck in the coals. We then got a volunteer, which really meant some poor first former was carried kicking and screaming to the room. He was tied to the chair and his arms and legs strapped in place. We showed him the poker in the fire and even took it out the fire to show him it was red hot. Then we blind folded him and also gagged him, as he was making a terrible noise. Now silently we brought another chair into the room and placed it next to the boy's right arm. We had a steak we had kept from lunch, we hadn't liked the steaks that day anyway. The steak was placed on the arm of the second chair without the boy's awareness. We had a second poker which was cold, room temperature that is. We told the boy we were about to place the hot poker on his arm and we then placed the hot poker on the steak at exactly the same time as the room temperature poker was placed on the boy's arm. Even with the gag in place you heard the boy scream and a bright red burn appeared immediately on his arm. We took off the blindfold and showed the boy we hadn't actually hurt him at all. Nevertheless there remained on this boy's arm a burn mark which became a scar for as long as I remember him at the university. As you can imagine, we all nearly got expelled but as we hadn't actually burnt him, and we could argue we were conducting experiments for our studies we were allowed to stay with serious cautions. That 'experiment' became famous on the campus and at several other universities. The conclusion was that as the mind was totally convinced, the body responded appropriately. The boy's mind had been told the arm was going to be burnt with a hot poker. It had seen the poker in the fire. It had felt the touch of the poker. It heard the sizzle of the burning flesh. It could even smell the burning flesh. All the boy's senses told his mind he was being burnt so the body acted accordingly and produced pain and a burn.

The point of this story is to explain that although I have told you 'the hound from Hell' is not real but a projection from that foul Demon's mind, the hound is so terrifying and so real that if it bites you, you will not be able to convince your mind it is not real. If it bites you in the throat you will probably die. You will suffer as though it was real. That is why I treated it as real." "So Steve, what about the Demon then" Cathy asked, "is that now dead?" "I am afraid not" Steve replied. "You can't kill a Demon, or at least I don't know how you can. You can send it back to where it came from though, but even that is not easy, and can be very dangerous. As I explained we were fighting a real demon but because it couldn't get to us due to the protective circle we were fighting a hound which was a projection into our minds. We hurt the projection not the demon. The chances are we have merely driven the demon away for now, but not back to Hell. It is however very unlikely that it will return tonight, if ever but I can't be sure yet. I need to talk to Peter and find out what the Satanic High Priest said to him. We must therefore spend the rest of the night in the circle to be on the safe side. Make up as comfortable a bed as possible with the blankets, sheets and pillows and try and get some sleep. You do not need to be vigilant, you can relax and sleep if possible." Liz threw her arms around Steve "You are a life saver Steve. I will never forget what you have done for me tonight." "Unfortunately this may not be over yet," said Steve "but we do live to fight another day." By 5am Steve had not felt any hostile presence for the rest of the night so he decided to leave and offered to drop Lauren off on the way. He checked with Cathy and she agreed to stay with Liz for the next two or three days, basically until Steve said they were safe.

CHAPTER 10

The Demon of Lust

Meanwhile, on Friday evening, back at The Pinnacle, Aleister had decided after Peter and Dame Alice left, to have an early night. If they were continuing to celebrate Yuletide all the coven members were making their own arrangements. It is also important, Aleister thought, that the members had their own free time and weren't totally dominated by the coven. The truth was that Aleister didn't give a damn for them but if they were kept happy he didn't have problems recruiting new members and protecting the future of the coven for Satan, and of course for himself. Right now Aleister wanted to address his own needs and was on his way up to Rachel's room. Aleister's role as High Priest meant that he had to perform sexual intercourse on many occasions as part of initiation ceremonies, to both men and women. But because he had to perform to an audience as part of a ceremony and to whoever the initiate was, he did not find it satisfying. He did of course have many opportunities for sexual release at the sexual rituals but like Dame Alice he often preferred to stay aloof and manage proceedings. As it was he found sexual intercourse didn't meet his needs. He can't really remember when it was that he had realised this. Whether he had lost his enthusiasm for sexual intercourse because of his role as High Priest or whether he had always been like that but didn't realise earlier, he wasn't sure. He was pleased however that Astaroth had answered his call and enabled him to perform as and when needed, whether he wanted to or not. It was extremely useful for him to have a Demoness of Love as their Patron Demon.

So he made his way up to Rachel's room. Rachel was 29 years of age and born in Hungary. She was about five foot two with dark brown hair, large dark eyes and a pretty face. She was a little overweight but mainly in the right places, curvy that is. She usually wore short skirts and loose blouses accentuating her ample cleavage. Because of her bad lisp and stammer she spoke very little which endeared her to Aleister even more. Because of Rachel's relationship to Aleister and the needs she fulfilled, Rachel had a special position in the Pinnacle household and therefore had more time to herself and more freedom, excepting she was confined to the house and grounds. Aleister didn't know whether Rachel enjoyed supplying his needs or whether she was a good actor. He didn't really care either way though, as long as she met his requirements. From Rachel's point of view, before she met Aleister she had been bullied and beaten by her own family and had spent most of her childhood and youth hiding the bruises.

Now she had her own room, the protection that came with pleasing Aleister and time to herself without any threats or physical violence. She knew there would never be physical violence from Aleister as he had no need of it. His power over her mind was such that Aleister could force Rachel to do anything he wanted without need of violence. Rachel however was prepared to do whatever Aleister wanted without force. It was an acceptable arrangement. The only thing that Rachel didn't like was that Aleister would come into her room without warning or without even knocking. Still it was a small price to pay as far as she was concerned. When Aleister walked in to her room this evening he found Rachel lying peacefully on her bed reading. She immediately stood up and Aleister removed his shoes, trousers and pants and laid down on Rachel's bed. Rachel aroused Aleister and then went down to him with her mouth. When Aleister was finished Rachel went to her basin and cleaned her teeth and gargled with mouthwash whilst Aleister got dressed. Aleister smiled at her and left. Not one word was said by either of them during Aleister's visit.

Aleister then went to his own room and after preparing for bed, telephoned Alice from his bedside phone. Alice explained that she had four coven members attending tomorrow evening at 9pm but she had included George even though he wasn't very experienced, it would in fact be only his third time in the circle. However she felt George was confident and would very much benefit from the experience. Aleister said he was satisfied and would see her tomorrow evening.

The next morning at The Pinnacle broke clear and bright, if a little cold, but then it was the 27th December. After his breakfast, Aleister had his coffee on the patio at the back of the house. He was looking at the lawn and considering that night's circle. After making up his mind he sent for Castor. When Castor arrived Aleister told him to organise the respraying of the two large circles plus the small circle at the eastern side of the main circle. Then the pentacle star itself. This meant that once the dew had evaporated and the grass was dry Castor would use white spray paint to highlight the circles and star, very much as they do on the sports grounds. It made it much easier for the coven members with the placement of the candles and the preparation of the protective circle. Aleister then asked Castor to make sure the cauldron is prepared and the fire lit and burning by 9pm latest. Aleister also wanted a few discreet garden lights on as it was a dark moon that night, in case the candles were blown out by the wind (Astaroth is often accompanied with a swirling wind).

Aleister then went over to the kitchens and told the staff to prepare food and drink for tonight in the lounge, for seven people, that is six guests plus himself. As well as the wine there must be tea and coffee and hot mulled wine at 8.30pm onwards and then food as well from 11pm onwards. The food must include hot snacks as the members will be cold. He suggested they include hot burgers, hotdogs and especially toasted home cooked bread with lots of melted cheese as that is always very popular. He then summoned Rachel and told her to tell the housemaids to ensure there was soap, shampoo and clean dry towels in the bathrooms for at least seven people. When Aleister was satisfied everything was arranged for the evening he went to his office and spent the rest of the morning in telephone conference with Dr John moving money and buying and selling stock.

By early evening, after an afternoon rest, Aleister had taken one of the besom brooms and chanting, he swept the area of the outside circles. Castor then prepared the cauldron in the centre whilst Aleister organised the altar and laid out the impedimenta for the night's ritual.

On the altar he put the black altar cloth with the images of the Sigil of Baphomet in the centre and the Sigils of Lucifer and Astaroth on either side. He placed a mounted inverted gold pentagram, two large black candles, a chalice, two small bowls and a large athame and of course a couple of boxes of matches. He went and collected ten stakes with sharpened pointed ends that could be pushed into the ground and on the top of each of the stakes were a metal saucer in bronze below a bronze candle stick holder. He walked around the circle and pushed a stake in the ground at each point of the pentagram and the remaining five stakes equidistant between them. He put four large coloured candles at the compass points, yellow at East, red at South, blue at West and green at North. These colours signified air, fire, water and earth respectively. In the remaining six candlesticks he placed large black candles. He put water in one bowl on the altar and salt in the other. It was nearly four o'clock and getting dark by the time he was finished preparing the circle. The guests were not due until nine o'clock which gave him five hours to spend in prayer and meditation in the Temple. He told Castor he would be in the Temple and to tell him when anyone arrived.

The guests started arriving from 8.30pm and all five members were there by 9pm, happily drinking coffee or hot mulled wine in the lounge. It was cold outside already and it was no time to drink cold wine. When they had each arrived Rachel had been instructed to take their domino or ceremonial gown in Alice's case, through to the bathrooms at the back. At nine o'clock Dame Alice led them to those rear bathrooms at the back of the house and they stepped outside into the cold about thirty minutes later. The scene was breathtaking. It was dark by then but the patio lights were on and a few garden lights, but they didn't take away from the magic of the ten large candles burning brightly around the circle. The candle flames wavered in the light breeze that had sprung up but the eye was drawn to the large cauldron in the centre of the circle spitting flames and sparks into the night air. The members were of course skyclad so walked towards the beautiful scene with a few shivers. If it hadn't been so dark a few would have shown more than a few goose bumps.

For all the beauty of the flaming cauldron and the flickering candles George couldn't take his eyes off Dame Alice. He hadn't seen

Dame Alice skyclad before. Alice was always very elegant and ladylike and normally wore very long dresses that came down to her ankles; now he knew why. Alice had long jet black hair that hung down her back and touched her bottom. But she also had thick body hair under her arms, between her legs and down her legs as well. She was in fact a beautiful woman so George could not understand why she didn't shave or at least trim her body hair. Aleister had now joined them and as they all stepped into the circles they pulled their dominos and gowns over their heads and George was able to concentrate on the matters at hand. Castor was now inside and had instructions to wait for Peter in the entrance hall. He was to take Peter with his domino to the same rear bathrooms and tell Peter that once he had showered he was to walk out skyclad to the circle at 10.30pm carrying his domino.

The four corners had already been allocated and the members went to their positions whilst Aleister and Alice prepared for the ritual. Aleister lit the altar candles and devoted the altar to Satan. They then blessed the salt and water and sprinkled them around the edge of the outer circle. But they didn't then call the corners in the usual way as Aleister was to conduct an invocation ritual. Aleister stood between the north end of the circle and the cauldron in the centre in his splendid ceremonial gown and addressed the members. "Our High Priestess has allowed George to join us tonight as we believe he will benefit from the experience. For his sake I will explain this ritual and our objective.

To summon Demons two types of rituals are practiced, invocation and evocation. Invocation comes from the Latin 'invocare' meaning to call on. It is where we invite a Demon to join us. The Demon is allowed unrestricted access into our circle, and communication and energies may well be exchanged. Evocation comes from the Latin 'evocatio' which means calling forth. Evocation is a magickal ritual forcing and commanding the Demon to attend. Because the ritual is threatening the Demon it is not invited into the same circle as the magician. The magician has a circle of protection around him or will call the Demon into a circle to restrict it and protect himself. Evocation is usually used by Christians and most of the old Grimoires were written for Christians to force or command Demons. Satanists mainly use invocation as their relationship with Demons is far more harmonious and the Demons will generally respond to invitation far better than force. George you may find this ritual very interesting as it is a combination of invocation and evocation. I will shortly call upon four Demons, invoking them into our circle. These are known Demons to us and therefore not a risk. If however Peter does have a Demon attached to him we don't know which Demon it is and therefore how safe it is. For that reason Peter will be in the separate circle where we will ask the Demon to remain."

Aleister turned his back on his colleagues and picked up the athame from the altar. He was facing George who was at the green candle for the north. "George, repeat three times after me, **we invoke the energy of the earth by calling upon the elemental demon BELIAL to join us in this circle.**" After George had repeated these words three times Aleister pointed the athame into the air and drew the ZD sigil in the air and cried out "**Lirach Tasa Vefa Wehl Belial.**" There was a draft of cold air and the cauldron flared up for a moment. Aleister then walked over to face Margaret by the yellow candle for the east and said "Margaret, repeat three times after me, **we invoke the energy of the air by calling upon the elemental demon and our patron demoness ASTAROTH to join us in this circle.**" Aleister again drew the sigil in the air and cried out "**Tasa Alora Foren Astaroth.**" Again there was a draft of cold air but it blew around the circle and Aleister feared it might extinguish the candles but the wind dropped and the candles remained alight. Aleister then walked over to face Tamsin by the red candle for the south. "Tamsin, repeat three times after me, **we invoke the energy of fire by calling upon the elemental demon FLEREOUS to join us in this circle.**" Aleister drew the sigil in the air and cried out "**Ganic Tasa Fubin Flereous.**" Once again the draft of cold air and the cauldron also flared for a moment. Aleister walked to the last corner where Dr John stood before the blue candle for the west. "John, repeat three times after me, **we invoke the energy of the water by calling upon the elemental demon ANDRAS to join us in this circle.**" Once more Aleister drew the ZD sigil in the air and cried out "**Entey Ama Andras Anay.**" The cold wind briefly returned but the cauldron seemed to flare up to counter the cold. Aleister then walked back to his position between the green north candle and the altar and called to Satan to witness this ritual in his honour crying "**Tasa Reme Laris Satan.**" The flames in the cauldron suddenly flared to about four feet and everyone stepped back but it died down as quickly.

At that moment, Peter appeared skyclad, walking over from the back of the house carrying his domino. Aleister called him over but told him not to step into the circle. He told Peter, on this occasion, to pull his domino on now so his hands are free. Aleister then without leaving the main circle, passed over to Peter the two small bowls from the altar. "Go over to the East and stand in the small circle. Sprinkle the Holy water slowly and carefully around the edge of the small circle, and then do the same with the salt. The small bowls can stay there with you in that circle." When Peter had finished, Aleister called to the demons present in the circle. He asked them to command the demon that had been seen with Peter, to join Peter in his circle. The demon was then to be commanded to identify itself. There was a great circular wind and a mist or haze that hid Peter from sight. Two of the candles had been blown out. As the mist cleared a bit, it became obvious Peter was not alone in his circle.

*A coven member steps into the circle 'skyclad'.

Aleister cried to the demon "In the name of Satan I demand you identify yourself." The demon was a vague outline still enshrouded in mist, obviously it did not intend to fully reveal itself. The demon screamed at Aleister in a high pitched wail, obviously unhappy that it had been commanded to obey. "I am no less than one of the seven princes of Hell. I represent one of the deadly sins. I was instrumental in the construction of the Temple of Solomon." "Ahh" Aleister said "you must be Asmodeus the demon of lust." "I am" it screamed "I demand you release me." "I will" Aleister replied "I only did this because I was unable to identify you. I need you to answer one question before I release you." "What is it you need to know?" the demon screamed. Aleister replied "What are your intentions? Do you intend to possess Peter?" "That is two questions" the demon screamed. "Alright, I need the answer to two questions and then I will release you" Aleister replied. The demon didn't answer at first. Aleister assumed it was thinking about the questions. Finally it said in its high pitched scream "I don't have a plan now. I was going to possess a female friend of Peter's but was driven away. I don't intend to possess Peter. It is not my plan." Aleister then said "We therefore have no quarrel Asmodeus. I will release you but be aware I have now identified you and should you possess Peter or any of my coven against their will, I will drive you back from whence you came. In the name of Satan I release you from that circle, you may join us or you may leave us." There was another high pitched scream and a strong wind and the outline of the demon vanished. Aleister looked at the others and said "We must firstly thank the demons for joining us and for commanding Asmodeus to co-operate. We must thank Satan for his presence and blessing. Then let us open these circles and go inside for hot bread and cheese and hot toddies, I am freezing and I am sure you are also."

Once they had warmed up in the bathrooms and changed back into their clothes they made their way to the main lounge at the front of the house. Aleister stopped Peter and told him that unfortunately he could not join them as he intends a teach-in and Peter has not yet been initiated. Aleister escorted Peter to the front door and promised he would invite him to join Dame Alice and himself, so they can discuss their findings of today. He said that Peter was not to worry about today, it went very well and he will explain everything to Peter at their meeting.

In the lounge, soft chairs were already in a circle and a spread of hot food and drinks was on tables close by. They each collected a plate and selected what they wanted to eat and drink and made themselves comfortable in one of the chairs. After a while Aleister returned and joined them. "Right then" Aleister said "I am sure you all have questions so let us make this a teach-in. Who wants to be first?" Margaret immediately said "You knew Asmodeus or at least you recognised his name, who exactly is he?" "What Asmodeus said to me is probably correct. In the Book of Tobit he is referred to as a King of Demons and he is also mentioned in Talmudic legends particularly in the construction of King Solomon's Temple, as Asmodeus proudly said to us this evening. Christians in the middle ages referred to him as the King of Nine Hells and he has been credited many times as the demon of lust, one of the seven deadly sins. He is also reported to be very jealous. He lusted after one particular woman and proceeded to kill seven of her new husbands, one after the other on their respective wedding nights. Obviously neither the woman nor Asmodeus intended to give up easily."

*** One of many very different
images of The demoness Astaroth.

"So why, Peter? Why has this demon decided to attach himself to Peter?" Tamsin asked. "I can't be sure of course, but I have a fairly good idea" Aleister said. "Think of the old Christian saying, speak of the Devil and he will appear. Well, a little simplistic but the idea is correct. If you think of any spirit a great deal, you can open a channel for it. In several religions men have gone into isolation, becoming hermits to spend all their time thinking about their deity. These men can become very close to their gods and become very powerful. The point is that, thinking a lot about a spirit may open a channel and you may be visited by that spirit. In this case Peter had just dedicated himself to Satan so was thinking a great deal about Satan and his demons. Combine that with the fact that we know Peter had not had a girlfriend for some time and I believe he was lusting after Carrie. I think Peter opened a channel for lust and attracted the demon for lust. I don't think there is any more to it than that."

"Is Peter safe and come to that is his friend Liz now safe?" Dr John asked. Aleister replied "They are both now much safer than they were, mainly because we now know the identity of the demon. Demons can be very dangerous to non Satanists. Demons consider us on their side and we can therefore invoke them easily and they will often grant our requests for help, as they did tonight. Christians, for example, have to force their co-operation by evocation and if they do not know what they are doing can get into a lot of trouble because demons do not appreciate being commanded or forced. Demons have their strengths but they also have their weaknesses. If you know the identity of the demon you know their weaknesses." "Okay," replied Dr John "so what are Asmodeus's weaknesses?" "He hates water and birds, they both remind him of God. If Peter or Liz became possessed by Asmodeus we immerse them in water." "Wow, High Priest, you make it sound so simple" Dr John said. "No easier than you make the stock market look, when you are managing my investments" Aleister replied. Dr John smiled "But I have a lot of help." "And you think I don't ?" Aleister countered.

"Can I ask a question please, High Priest?" George asks. "Of course George, go ahead." "What words and what language was it that you shouted to invoke the demons tonight?" George asked. "That is a very good question George, but I can only partly answer it. The words to call the demons are known as ENNs. They are sentences but of an unknown demonic tongue. The first actual written recording was by Alexander Willit in about 1550AD. Several Satanists have been given these call words by demons they have been working with and we have found that the same call words have been given to different Satanists working with the same demon. Most of the time we only have the call words and no understanding yet but there have been breakthroughs. This evening I called the demon Flereous using the ENNs: Ganic Tasa Fubin Flereous. We have been told these words stand for Fire protect the flame, Lord Flereous. That is why we call the demon Flereous in the south quarter, for the red candle, for the element of Fire."

"Is that it, any more questions?" Aleister said. "Well yes, I would like to ask one other question but it's very personal and I would like to ask it of Dame Alice" George said. "Go ahead George" Alice replied. "Well when we walked to the circle we were all skyclad. I noticed our High Priestess was covered in body hair. Dame Alice, you are a very beautiful lady, and that amount of body hair detracts from your beauty. I can only imagine there is a reason why you do not trim or shave your body hair. Is there a Satanic reason?" "No George, it is a personal reason. Every month I work a spell for youth. It delays the ageing process, but there are certain rules that must be followed with this spell working and one of them requires me not to cut or shave any of my body hair under any circumstances whatsoever. This is a common rule in several spells and certain religions.

In Judaism the traditional side curls on Jewish men are known as payos. In the Bible, in Leviticus chapter 19 verse 27 it states that a man must not cut the hair at the side of his head. The Rastafaris wear their hair in dreadlocks and they refer to the biblical prohibition against cutting hair and they also associate it with strength believing, like Samson, their strength lies in the length of their hair. In Sikhism they believe hair is a gift from God and therefore must not be cut in any way. In the Amish there is a major distinction between a beard and a moustache. They say that the Bible has many references to beards such as Psalm 133 verse 2, but they associate moustaches with the military, so they are banned. The point that I am making is that body hair can be significant with spiritual matters especially with spells." "Do you believe the spell for youth is working, does it make you feel younger?"

George asked. Aleister interrupted them by saying "You judge for yourself George, Dame Alice is seventy three." George turned and looked at Dame Alice with total shock in his eyes. "Dame Alice, That is amazing, I thought you were about forty."

Aleister then said "I think that is a good positive point to close our meeting on. Dame Alice, I would ask you to contact Peter and Carrie and arrange for all three of you to meet me here tomorrow night at 9pm. I want to hear from you Alice, how Carrie is coming along with her preparation for initiation. I also want to talk to Peter about what we established tonight and whether he is ready for initiation, I have some doubts. Then we have a full meeting here of all members next Saturday at 9pm. That is the 3rd of January and we have to plan and prepare for the Wednesday night 7th January which is St. Winebald Day. We will be initiating Peter and Carrie on that night. We must also start planning for Candlemass which closely follows on the 2nd February. We have to prepare our sacrifice and also discuss the spiritual gifts and powers we will ask Satan for, for certain members. I will see you tomorrow Alice and the rest of you next Saturday."

Aleister stood up and then showed his guests out. As he was walking upstairs he realised the invocations had taken a lot from him and he was exceptionally tired. He called for Castor and asked him to take a bottle of Chablis on ice and two glasses to Rachel's room. After Aleister had showered he went into Rachel's room. Because of Castor bringing the wine, she was now expecting Aleister. However after a glass of wine, Aleister only wanted to curl up next to Rachel and sleep. He just felt like company that night and Rachel would be undemanding.

CHAPTER 11

Living with a Demon

Steve Conners woke up on Sunday morning at about 8am but only because his alarm woke him, he had had only two hours sleep. He was worried about Liz and Cathy and needed to make some phone calls. He was pleased with the outcome of the previous night, but needed to follow it up to ensure Liz's safety. He was physically drawn to Liz but was aware of the big age difference, 26 years in fact, so didn't want to pursue it unless she gave him signals. Steve lived alone, he did have dates with ladies occasionally but the relationship often only lasted a few days or nights to be more accurate. He hadn't 'met the right one yet' as his mother would have said. The truth was, that he lived for his Pagan religion and only worked enough to pay the bills. The rest of the time he studied and practiced his beliefs. His Christian friends said to him that Christianity would be much stronger if Christians had the same commitment and moral fortitude as he had. That being said he paid a great price; not being able to work more and not having the funds to settle down with a family. A bit late now but he still hoped the right lady would come along and if that happened he knew the Goddess would show him the way forward. He was fifty four now but still good looking and fairly fit. Steve was five foot ten with blond hair with a slight touch of auburn colouring, he blamed that on his twenty five per cent Irish blood. He had green eyes that were always liked by the ladies and a strong physique with a minimal middle age spread. He dressed casually but was always clean and smart.

Lying in bed and worrying about Liz he realised he needed to do something about it. He got up and after making a real cup of coffee, from coffee beans that is, definitely not instant, he telephoned Peter. "Morning Peter, its Steve Conners. Sorry to ring so early on a Sunday morning but I am worried about Liz and need to hear what the Satanic High Priest said. I assume you have managed to talk to him about this demon that attacked Liz." Peter then proceeded to tell Steve everything that had happened regarding this demon. He told Steve about his visit to Aleister and what Aleister had said. He then told Steve about the invocation ritual and the details of what happened then. "I can't tell you anymore than that yet Steve because Aleister said he will contact me to come round for a meeting with him. He will then tell me what exactly happened last night and where we go from there. Aleister doesn't seem at all worried and now he knows what demon this is, I get the feeling he can handle it." "Okay, just phone me on my mobile phone when you have seen this Satanic High Priest, and tell me everything he said. I won't be at home so it's no use ringing my house. I need to know where we stand and whether we should be making plans to protect ourselves" replied Steve. Peter promised he would ring Steve immediately after he had seen Aleister.

Steve then rang Liz "Hi Liz, its Steve, I am sorry to disturb you, you haven't had much sleep. Since we left you and Cathy, how has it been?" "That's fine Steve. It's been okay, no disturbances at all. Just that neither of us could relax enough to actually sleep" Liz said. "Has Cathy definitely agreed to stay with you for the next two days and nights?" Steve asked. "Yes, no problem, she has promised to stay with me night and day until you say it's okay to leave." "That's good" Steve said "I won't be happy that you are safe until I know that this demon has been sent back to Hell. If Cathy is definitely there, she can also be your chaperone. If you are happy and you can make a bed up for me, I intend to move in until this situation is resolved. Are you okay with that?" "Yes that's great. I don't think I will need a chaperone but it's nice that you thought of that" Liz replied. Steve then said "I will turn up this afternoon and will bring my box of tricks in case we have problems. As you two can't go out is there anything you want me to bring with me?" Steve heard her asking Cathy and then Liz said "Some fresh milk and bread. Otherwise we are fine and will see you later."

Later in the day Steve packed his bag with clothes and toiletries, together with a second bag containing his Pagan impedimenta and made his way to Liz's flat.

Earlier that Sunday morning Aleister woke up confused. He was highly sexually aroused. He was lying on his back and when he looked down he saw the top of Rachel's head under his bedclothes. He never slept in anyone else's bed. He had intended to leave Rachel's bed and return to his own to sleep but had obviously slept there all night. It was the first time he had actually slept with a woman. He had to admit, as he relaxed back in the bed and let Rachel do her thing, it was a hell of a way to wake up in the morning. Rachel was probably taking a big risk and he was sure she knew that. He hadn't asked her to do this and it wasn't usual for him to want this morning arousal. If he had been upset her punishment could have been severe. As it was, he was happy and when he finished he got up and walked to the shower in his own room with a spring in his step. As he shaved and dressed Aleister thought through the meetings that evening with Dame Alice, Carrie and Peter. Later he rang Alice and asked her to arrive a little before the others, maybe 8pm. That way they can talk in private first.

Dame Alice arrived as expected at 8pm and Castor showed her into the lounge. She looked very attractive and very elegant and nothing like her seventy three years. Her jet black hair shone with health and flowed down over her shoulders to her waist. The low front of the dress showed her subtle cleavage, whilst the silky dress hugged her curves and the length meant it nearly met her expensive looking black high heels. Her make up was perfect and there was a sparkle in her eyes. Her gifts from Satan had been the spells for youth which really did work for her. In return she devoted her life to Satan and worked hard for the coven, providing support for all the members. Aleister was relaxing in a comfy chair with a glass of the Chablis he never finished last night. It was re-chilled and still tasted divine. Aleister hadn't stood up for Alice when she walked in, she was like part of the family and Aleister treated her as such. It was his way of complimenting her. He just waved her to a seat and Castor leant down and asked her what she wanted to drink. "I'll have a glass of whatever Aleister is drinking."

Once she was settled and also had a glass of cold Chablis, Aleister asked her about her day and how she felt the ritual had gone the night before. They discussed the ritual in detail and made mental notes for the future. "How is Carrie coming along with her preparation for initiation?" Aleister asked. Alice replied "I have no worries or concerns about Carrie, Aleister." "Do I read into that, that you do have worries and concerns about Peter?" "Yes absolutely. Peter may be ready one day but not in the very near future" Alice confirmed. "I agree totally" Aleister said "I have been watching him and he is in real trouble. The demon Asmodeus has taken up residence at Peter's flat and steps into Peter with ease whenever it suits. Asmodeus is not threatening Peter at present in any way, it is just taking advantage and enjoying the ride. However we have to remember what this devil is capable of; it murdered seven men at one point just because of jealousy. I cannot bind this demon if Peter is welcoming it. As you know Peter has to want it removed before I can act and the problem is, Peter is enjoying the ride as well."

"What do you plan to do Aleister?" Alice asked. "Carrie and Peter are due to arrive shortly. I want you to take Carrie into the small lounge and spend a little time with her. Do whatever you can to make sure Carrie is ready for her initiation and please remember I do need her initiated and ready to prepare Gwendoline for her sacrifice. I will talk to Peter in here. I will not interfere but I do need to make sure Peter does understand what he is playing with. I also need to express on Peter that he has to call for help when he needs it. I will explain to Peter how easy it is to drive this demon away, but he has to ask for it."

At that point Aleister heard the main front doors opening and as the lounge doors had been deliberately left open he saw Carrie and Peter walk in and be greeted by Castor. Castor however then hurried into the lounge and explained that Dr John was waiting to speak to Aleister on his main phone in the office. Aleister said to the three of them to wait a moment and he'll be back. Dr John was Aleister's financial advisor and had to tell Aleister that he had bad premonitions about a particular stock that Aleister had a lot of money invested in. Dr John urgently needed Aleister's okay to lay off all that stock but of course not too quickly so as to scare the market. Aleister had total trust in Dr John and told him to go ahead. When Aleister returned to the main lounge he immediately saw the expression on Peter's face. Aleister knew at once that Peter was currently possessed by Asmodeus and by the way Peter was looking at Carrie could probably see Carrie completely naked. Aleister marched towards Peter and shouted at him "Peter I don' really care what you do in your own home but in my home you show me respect." Aleister's tone then became far more angry and aggressive "Asmodeus I am now talking to you," he shouted "get the Hell out of Peter and get the Hell out of my house. If you remain I will send you back to where you came from." There was a squeal like a pig makes when the farmer pushes it away with his boot and Peter's expression changed to one of annoyance, like a small child. Aleister turned and looked at Alice, "Dame Alice, you and Carrie go and talk in the small lounge. Tell Castor whatever it is you want to drink or eat. And you Peter will stay and talk to me."

Aleister waved Peter to a seat and once the two ladies had left them, Aleister looked hard at Peter and said "Peter you had better tell me what is happening with you, and please remember I am able to oversee you at any time and sometimes do." "High Priest, I am glad of this chance to talk to you about what is happening to me. I am very much aware that I have a presence with me nearly all the time. I would have expected it to be a frightening experience but it isn't. It's hard to explain; although the presence appears to be around me most of the time it's not in a specific place or position. I've heard of people talking of a demon on your shoulder that whispers in your ear, but it's not like that at all. I am just aware of a presence with me most of the time and thoughts seem to come into my head which I am sure are not my thoughts. To add to that, occasionally it steps into me and I can then see and feel what it can and I guess the other way around as well. In other words it can see and feel what I do. I have the feeling it wants to experience what I can and do. I need to ask you what happened Saturday night. I know you found a demon with me but can you tell me more please. Is this dangerous for me?"

"A demon is always dangerous" Aleister replied. "It has no conscience and no interest in mankind. You can't kill it and normally it's not easy to send back to where it came from. Demons don't like most humans and are therefore antagonistic to us and will attack us for very little reason. They especially dislike Christians because there is a history of Christian preachers banning and binding demons. Satanists are the only group that are able to work with demons, basically because demons answer to Satan as we do, so there is some affinity there. Christians and other religious groups have to evoke demons, which means force and control them, and if anything goes wrong the demon will then attack the humans, angry that it was forced to obey. Satanists are able to invoke demons which means invite them and they will often respond to us and willingly join us and sometimes even help us. Like humans, each demon is different and it is very important to identify the demon. We are then able to understand that demon and often, why it is there and how to send it home if that became necessary." Peter then asked "Did you identify this demon on Saturday night and if so, does that tell you who it is and why it is here?" "Yes, yes and yes" said Aleister.

"The demon" Aleister said "is Asmodeus. This is a very well known demon, which is good, because as it is well known we know a lot about it. We can therefore deduce its likely behaviour patterns and more importantly, how to control or expel it. Asmodeus is a King in its own world so it demands to be respected. Show it respect if you can. It is famous because it was instrumental in the building of King Solomon's Temple and it is one of the keeper's of the seven deadly sins, in its case, 'Lust'. It is not for me to decide your life Peter, you haven't even been initiated yet. So you must do what you want but this demon will have an effect on you and only you can decide to accept or reject it. How do you feel about its presence generally?" Peter replied "I have to admit I am enjoying it. It makes sense now you have told me about it being the keeper of 'Lust', because I am continuously horny and when it is inside me I can see the ladies as though they were naked. It is quite revealing and enjoyable of course, well at least with the young ones. I have never been clairvoyant or any such gifts so it is exciting to be able to experience something from the 'other side'. I would like to continue to experience this for the present but would like to be able to come to you if I was in trouble. Is that possible?" Peter asked.

"Yes" Aleister replied "that is possible. I wouldn't want you playing this game approaching initiation, it would add further complications. However we have already decided you are not yet ready for initiation and need further time to prepare. So that being the case, I have no objections to your proposal as long as you have put this behind you when you are ready for initiation. We must all go through different spiritual experiences as we progress and grow, and it is not for me to set boundaries unless I see major risks to my coven." Peter replied "Thank you High Priest. Can you also please explain why this demon came to me and not to someone else. It's not as though I called it." "There, I think you are totally wrong Peter. I think you have very much called this demon. Think about it. You admitted you hadn't had sex for sometime, you were lusting after Carrie, and then Liz and at the same time joining my coven and calling upon Satan and his demons. You opened a channel to the other-side for demons and lust. Who else would respond than the demon for Lust itself, Asmodeus."

***Asmodeus, referred to as the King of the Nine Hells and as one of the seven princes of hell. This was because he represents one of the seven deadly sins. Asmodeus is the demon of lust.

"Put like that it does make sense" Peter said "so we know the demon, we know why he is here and how he got here but you said if you knew the demon, you would know how to send it back if it became necessary." Aleister replied "I did and I do. I did say if I knew the demon and you're right we know it is Asmodeus, I would know how to send it back. Asmodeus has a fear of birds and water. The Christians say it is because it reminds it of God. I don't think that is true but it does nevertheless hate birds and water. It is therefore very simple for us to send it back. If Asmodeus takes permanent possession of you we can totally immerse you in water. It wouldn't even need to be Holy water, any water will do. You need to hold your breath and we need to make sure you are totally immersed and the demon doesn't try to come into us, to stop it being sent back. Peter, I am making this sound very simple but remember who I am. I am a Satanic High Priest, a high level adept, an Ipsissimus. Experiment by all means. By experimenting we have all learned and gained experience but remember you are not even initiated yet. Demons can be very dangerous, they have no conscience. We know for a fact this demon killed seven men just because of jealousy for a woman it could never have anyway."

"Can I ask two more things please High Priest?" "Yes, go ahead Peter." "What about my friend Liz, is she now safe?" Aleister replied "Yes, I think so. If the demon has taken residence with you, it's not with her. So unless there is a change of your relationship with the demon, Liz can return to normality. However do not go around to Liz's flat, that would be tempting providence or should I say tempting the demon. You had another question?" "Yes, High Priest, can I tell Steve, the Pagan High Priest what you have told me? He is worried about Liz and wanted to know what you had found out." "There is currently no conflict between Steve and I, as far as I know. Yes that would be fine" Aleister said. Peter thanked Aleister very much. As Peter left, Aleister promised to 'keep an eye on him' and he would invite him back, to talk further regarding his progress to initiation.

Shortly afterwards as Aleister was preparing to go to his room, Dame Alice and Carrie arrived back in the entrance hall. Aleister walked over to them and could see they were both happy with their discussions. "You both look pleased. I take it your talk went well." Aleister looked at Alice "Are you confident Carrie is going to be ready for her initiation in only ten days time?" Alice replied "Yes, very much so." Looking at Carrie like a proud Mum would have, she continued "remember Carrie has been with us for three months now and unlike

Peter has been to many meetings. Also she has always been very focused on her goals." "Excellent" Aleister said "We are meeting again Saturday 3rd January so can discuss any last minute worries, but it sounds like you don't have any." Aleister walked them both to the front doors and said "Goodnight Ladies. Alice I will keep a close watch on Peter and will ring you if we have any problems in that direction." They said goodnight to Aleister and left.

When Peter got back to his flat he telephoned Steve on his mobile. Even though it was now nearly midnight Steve answered immediately. Peter told Steve everything Aleister had said. Steve was however still worried for Liz. "Aleister may have control over that demon, but Peter you certainly don't. Frankly I think you are mad doing what you are doing and I believe very strongly you should go back to Aleister in the morning and tell him you have changed your mind and can he send the demon back to where it came from." Peter replied "I don't want to, Steve and any-rate I am at work in seven hours time. I will think about what you said Steve. Sleep well and thank you."

Steve was in Liz's second bedroom and he could hear the two girls talking in the other bedroom, so he banged on their door and they said he could come in. Steve explained everything that Peter had said. "I must admit I expected that when the Satanic High Priest found out who the demon was and therefore knew how to handle it, he would send it packing. But I guess that's the difference between us and them. He has let the demon stay with Peter and Peter seems to think he can play cat and mouse with it without getting eaten. I hope Peter is right and he will be okay. The other problem is that, if it goes wrong with Peter and the demon breaks away from him, it might come over here, and we might not get any warning either. I think, Liz, you are probably still at risk, with very little warning, if any. I feel I should stay here until this is resolved. How do you feel about me in your spare bedroom for a while?" Steve asked. Liz replied immediately "If you are prepared to do that and if you can spare the time, I would be very happy for you to be here. I would be very pleased for you to stay anytime but right now I do need you here, especially if you think I could be at risk." "Okay," Steve replied "in the morning, when its daylight, I will go back to my house and pack a proper bag. I've only got an overnight bag at present. Maybe in the morning, you two can look at what provisions we have here and make a list of further things needed and give it to me at breakfast time. I'll leave you in peace, see you both at breakfast."

Once Steve had left their bedroom Cathy said "I didn't want to ask this in front of Steve but do you really need me as chaperone? I am pleased to help you and will stay as long as you need me but the truth is I still don't have a job and need to continue job hunting really urgently. What I'm trying to say, is that Steve can protect you far better than me, so if you don't actually need me, can I go home and get on with my job hunting?" "If I didn't like or trust Steve it would be a problem, but it's not. I will enjoy Steve here but I can't show too much enthusiasm, can I?" Liz replied. "Okay" Cathy said "that's sorted. We'll tell Steve I'll be shooting off immediately he gets back with his things and the shopping. I think we should try and get some sleep now." Liz turned off the main light but kept the bedside light on and they both snuggled under the duvet in Liz's big double bed.

Steve returned to the second bedroom which now seemed very empty. He was dying for a stiff drink but hadn't brought any with him. A double brandy would go down really well right now. He made a mental note to pack a bottle of brandy and whisky with his clothes. A book by a favourite author would be a good idea as well. He thought a week in the second bedroom was going to seem like a long time.

CHAPTER 12

The Initiation

It was Monday morning. 'I must have fallen asleep eventually' Steve thought as he woke up. He just remembered tossing and turning. His head filled with Peter and his demon one minute and two pretty dark eyed girls in the other room, the next. As any man will tell you, sexual frustration is the worst thing for getting to sleep. Add to that the worry of a real live demon that could turn up any time, in your head or even in the flesh and you've got the best prescription for insomnia yet. Steve's greatest worry was that Peter probably had to go to work this morning. So was the demon going with him or did it do something else until he got home. Still he would find out soon enough and he had survived another sleepless night in the meantime. It will get better, it has to.

He crawled out the bed and into the shower. It did at least wake him up and then a shave and some eggs for breakfast. He was just finishing his third boiled egg, when the girls appeared. Well he will need sustenance to fight demons, won't he, he thought. The girls sat down at the kitchen table opposite him and asked about his night. He lied and said he had slept well. He couldn't say he was sexually frustrated or that he was worried about a demon turning up, could he? They immediately said they hadn't managed to get to sleep for ages. Still they felt much safer with him next door. They went on to explain that Cathy needs to get back to her flat. She has bills to pay and still no job, so they had decided, if it's okay with him, for Cathy to go home.

If Steve needs to leave at any time, Cathy will come back and keep Liz company. With most of Steve's enthusiasm aimed at Liz, having Liz in the flat on her own didn't seem too bad an idea, as long as he can hide his feelings for her. At any-rate the girls had already decided, so Cathy would shoot off when he returned with his luggage. Steve confirmed he had no problems with that and said he would leave to get his things after breakfast. When he did arrive back at his house Steve rang every member of his coven and told them about Peter and his demon and that he was currently staying at Liz's flat to protect her in the event that the demon tried to attack her. He told everyone he would be contactable on his mobile and he would contact them if he needed the cavalry. He got lots of offers to help and to relieve him if he needed a break or if he just needed some shopping dropped in. But then that is exactly what a coven is all about. He told them there weren't any meetings or workings arranged but if he needed a cone of power or some other support he would ask Lauren to organise it.

In the meantime Peter had left his flat to go to work at the café on Brighton's seafront. Peter felt strange. The demon was still around. It wasn't inside him but he could feel the presence all the time. The demon wasn't controlling him, Peter was making his own decisions and the demon was coming along for the ride. He was happy with that state of affairs but he had noticed that each time the demon came inside him it seemed to stay a little longer. He would monitor the time it stayed inside him. Otherwise he was enjoying the experience as the demon's presence gave Peter an awareness he had never before experienced. He had heard that artists who paint or write music sometimes benefit greatly by being high on drugs. Their consciousness and awareness changes and they become sensitive to their surroundings, that then is inspirational to their creative juices. Peter felt the demon gave him a shift of reality that he could only relate to taking drugs. It was therefore addictive as well, but Peter swore to monitor and control the experience and he vowed to tell Aleister if he was losing control.

*** This is King Baal (or Bael), he has three heads, a toad,
a man and a cat. He is head of infernal powers, the first
King of Hell with Estates in the East. He commands 66 legions.

The next meeting of the Satanic coven was on Saturday 3rd
January. Although this included all the members together with those
yet to receive initiation, it was only a meeting. It was a get-together to
discuss plans and the coven's future diary. The main topics were the
initiation of Carrie in four days time, on St. Winebald Day and the
sacrifice of a virgin on Candlemass on 2nd February. Dame Alice spent
time with Carrie going through the ritual and what was expected of
her and then Tamsin introduced Gwendoline to Carrie. Carrie would
be responsible after St. Winebald Day for preparing Gwendoline for
her ritual. However Carrie was unable to fully focus on Gwendoline
yet, with her own initiation so close at hand and explained as much to
Tamsin. Tamsin fully understood and did comment that it was unusual
to have both rituals so close together. Tamsin said she would happily
re-introduce Gwendoline to her after 7th January. The meeting broke
up and all the members left giving their best wishes for Carrie at her
initiation.

On Tuesday night 6th January Carrie did not sleep well. She just couldn't stop thinking of her initiation. She wasn't getting second thoughts, this was what she had been waiting for, for some time. To Carrie this was the beginning of her road to power and success. Nevertheless every aspect of her initiation kept running through her head and it meant that Wednesday morning she had had very little sleep. She knew she wouldn't be able to cope with a day's work and the ritual that night, so she rang in sick, telling her boss that she had a stomach bug and would be off Wednesday and Thursday. She then turned over in bed and finally went to sleep. Later she got up and had a late breakfast. Then she checked her domino was clean and dry, and then read and re-read her oath so that she knew it by heart. During the afternoon she lay down for a nap and did fall off to sleep again, so by early evening she was well rested. Although Carrie normally prefers to shower, she had a soak in the bath instead and after washing her beautiful blond hair so that it shone, she dressed and took her domino and hand bag and climbed into her car for the journey to The Pinnacle.

It was still only 8.30pm when she pulled up outside the green entrance gates to The Pinnacle, so she was half an hour early. The gates nevertheless immediately started to open and she drove up the long dark driveway to the house. As she got closer to the house the lights automatically switched on and although there were at least a dozen cars already parked, she still managed to find a space close to the front steps. Carrie picked up her handbag and domino from the car and climbed up the steps. As she walked inside the entrance doors, Dame Alice came hurrying towards her and greeted her with open arms followed by a big hug that made her feel really welcome, like she was on her first proms night. It was a lovely feeling for Carrie. She desperately wanted to be part of this exclusive family and taste the riches and success of the coven. Alice said "This is a very special night for you. Aleister will talk to you in the circle about all the points we have already discussed at length. You don't need to worry or think about anything particular, just let the evening and the other members carry you through the celebration."

Dame Alice then led her down the corridor and up the rear stairs so they came out at the bathrooms without going through the Temple. Alice took her into the bathrooms and said "The other members are already here and the circle is prepared. When we walk into the circle together they will call the corners and close the circle. Aleister will talk to you. You will read your oath and sign it in blood. Aleister will then drink your blood which binds him and the coven to you and you to the coven in blood. You will then turn your back to the members in the circle and face the altar. Then lean over the altar towards the Goat of Mendes and Aleister will enter you. It is important that he orgasms but he will be quick. It is not a sexual act as such, so neither of you will be expecting enjoyment or fulfilment. Because of this there is no foreplay and I hope you have remembered to use a cream to ensure you are not made uncomfortable. After that you are also bonded to the coven by body. I am sure you see the significance of the body and blood bonding. By submitting to this you are making a declaration of total servitude to Satan and to the coven. You must remember that everyone in the circle has had to go through this ritual; you will have their understanding and support. You will then be given a name in Satan by the High Priest and will then always be addressed by that name. We will open the circle and you are then an initiate of the strongest and most powerful coven in the South of England.

We need to prepare and remove our clothes. I see you have your domino and my gown is in here. We carry these to the circle and slip them on when we step into the circle, as before." Alice then gave Carrie another very warm and very emotional hug and said "You will be very blessed." They walked into an inner bathroom, removed their clothes and with their robes over their arms walked to the door of the Temple and stepped through. All the lights in the Temple were off. However around the external perimeter of the circle there were about two dozen large black candles with their flames dancing in the drafts of the Temple. These were further echoed by large black candles with dancing flames on the altar and above the altar was the image of the Goat of Mendes in spot lights. In this mesmerizing atmosphere the two beautiful ladies stepping out of the bathroom made quite an impact as they walked to the circle. Both were tall, elegant and beautiful but Alice was sallow skinned, had long jet black hair and a great deal of black body hair, whilst Carrie was pale skinned, had long blond hair and her body hair was shaved and trimmed. Every member of the coven was transfixed, watching them approach the circle, thinking how magical this was.

Alice and Carrie stopped at the edge of the circle, both looking at Aleister. Aleister turned and looked back at them. He was in full regalia, a gloriously decorated ceremonial gown, a gold crown on his head with an inverted pentagram on the front and about his neck a gold necklace with a beautifully painted Baphomet image on a disc. He smiled and nodded which Dame Alice took as permission to enter the circle. Carrie followed her lead and both ladies stepped into the circle pulling their robes over their heads and down over their bodies. They both stood quietly in the centre of the circle whilst their colleagues called the corners. But as was usual for this coven, when it was an initiation ritual they called the Kings of Hell. In the East they named Uricus calling Renich Tasa Uberaca Biasa Uricus. In the South they named Amaymon calling Ganic Tasa Fubin Amaymon. In the West they named Paymon calling Jedan Tasa Hoet Paymon. In the North they named Egyn calling Lirach Tasa Vefa Egyn. Then the High Priest looked up at the Dark Circle on the ceiling and cried out "This ritual is before the almighty Satan and in the presence of our Patron Demoness Astaroth. It is an initiation to bond our new member to the coven in the service of Satan."

Aleister then looked at Carrie and said to her "You must bond to the coven, like that of a family, putting the best interests of the coven and its members, first in your life. The initiation ritual is permanent. Your interests and goals should be in harmony with the coven's interests and goals. Above all you must be totally and completely dedicated to Satan and that is for life." Just like at her dedication the High Priest and High Priestess stepped towards her and Dame Alice held her hand whilst Aleister pricked her finger with a small athame. He then squeezed her finger until a few drops of blood fell into the small bowl he held under her hand. Dame Alice had picked up the oath from the altar which was exactly the same as the copy she had been practicing with at home. Carrie then read the oath aloud "I Carrie Tanning before almighty Satan and our patron demoness Astaroth and before all the members present solely swear of my own free will, that I will keep all those things secret that are entrusted to me as such. I promise to work for Satan and to support his army and apply my energy and those powers entrusted to me to destroy all enemies of Satan. I will also apply my entrusted powers to help and assist any coven member who needs my assistance at any time, knowing they will do the same for me. I swear this on my life and may these powers turn against me should I break this solemn oath. Lord Satan, Lord of all demons and powers of hell, may you find me worthy." The High Priest held out a pen for Carrie which she took. She then placed the oath on the altar and dipping the pen in her blood she signed the oath.

Aleister picked up from the altar the chalice, which had been filled with red wine, and poured some of the wine into the small bowl which had Carrie's blood in it. He then put the bowl to his lips and drank it all. He looked at Carrie and said "We are joined in blood and must now be joined in body." Aleister stepped aside and Carrie stepped forward and placed herself across the altar towards the Baphomet so that she was lying on the altar with her feet on the floor. Aleister stepped behind her so Carrie was partially hidden from the other members by Aleister. He raised her domino at the back and entered her. After a few minutes Aleister cried out which was accompanied by a great swirl of wind and the outline of Astaroth formed, hovering above the altar. The wind suddenly increased and all the candles were blown out. There remained only the two spot lights on the Baphomet image for lighting. Aleister and Carrie adjusted their gowns and Aleister then picked up the matches and went around the circle relighting all the candles. When this was done Aleister stood before Carrie, placed his hands on her head and blessed her in the name of Satan. "You are now an initiate in Satan and will be henceforth called Hecate. Hail Satan" he cried. "Hail Satan" the whole circle cried. The circle now called the corners thanking all present and opened the circle. Dame Alice went over and put the main lights on and then everyone walked to the bathrooms to change. They then slowly made their way to the lounge, each one taking the time to congratulate Hecate.

***King Paimon is one of the Kings of Hell.
He commands 200 legions of demons and when
Paimon appears the conjuror must allow him to
ask what he wishes and be answered.

Downstairs in the lounge several members were congregating around Aleister including Hecate herself. They were all keen to know who Hecate was. When everyone had helped themselves to food and drink and was settled in the comfy armchairs, Aleister decided it was a good time to explain.

"Hecate" Aleister began "was a human mortal princess in the 14th century who is believed to have committed suicide but was raised from the dead by Artemis. For those of you not yet familiar with Greek mythology I will tell you the story. Leto, a Titan Goddess, daughter of Coeus and Phoebe became a favourite lover of Zeus. However Zeus decided to marry Hera whilst Leto was pregnant with Zeus's child. Although the pregnancy was consummated before the marriage Hera was nevertheless jealous of Leto. Leto, hunted by Hera, had to run away and gave birth to Artemis on the Island of Ortygia. What happened to her mother affected her so badly that when Artemis grew up she asked Zeus to grant her eternal chastity and virginity. She never had any lovers but devoted herself to nature and hunting, rejecting love and marriage. Hecate, saved by Artemis, became associated with herbology and specialised in plants that were poisonous and hallucinogenic. In the Malleus Maleficarum of 1468, Hecate was praised and revered by the witches for her work.

Hecate was known as the Goddess of Sorcery, and of fertility in Greek and Egyptian culture. She was considered very beautiful but is often portrayed as having three heads. This is because she was a moon goddess and her kingdoms were threefold, that is earth, sky and sea. Hence she had to be able to look in three directions at once." "Does that mean she actually had three heads High Priest?" Tamsin asked. "No, not at all" Aleister replied "The images that are often portrayed of most Gods, Demons and Angels are symbolic. They usually look nothing like their portrayed images. The image is a symbolic statement of their character or power. For example angels don't have wings but are portrayed to have them to differentiate them from us and remind us they can fly. The image a demon portrays tells us its character or preferences, not what it looks like. Jesus is often referred to as the Lamb of God so Satan is referred to as The Goat of Mendes. He is therefore portrayed as a Goat but again that is purely symbolic. Satan is the most beautiful creation ever. Read Ezekiel chapter 28 verses 12 – 15. Satan is the highest of all angels the most beautiful ever created. Hecate is beautiful, she doesn't have three heads or I wouldn't have named Carrie after her."

Aleister then looked at Dame Alice. "Our next important ritual is less than four weeks away. Dame Alice please talk to Hecate and arrange a time for the two of you to meet. You can come here if you wish, it doesn't matter. You will then have to meet Tamsin with, of course, Gwendoline. Gwendoline must quickly get used to Hecate and learn to trust her. Make sure Gwendoline is taking her night time medication and increase it a little. Not too much, I don't want her resistant to it, just used to it. Any problems Dame Alice, speak to me about it." Everyone was now beginning to get tired and they were making their congratulations and farewells to Hecate and moving to the entrance hall. It was still a dark moon and therefore very dark and cold outside. They were all pleased to get back to their warm homes.

CHAPTER 13

When we least expect it

It was Thursday 8th January the day after the initiation. Peter was disappointed that he hadn't been initiated but Carrie, or Hecate as she was now called, had been a member longer than him, so he hoped his turn would come soon. Also there were two lady members, Sheila and Veronica, who hadn't been initiated yet. Maybe Aleister was going to arrange an initiation ritual for all three of them together. In the meantime Peter felt he was coping well with his visitor. He really enjoyed the amazing insight he had when Asmodeus stepped into him. He didn't think of it as possession because Peter felt he was in charge, he decided what he wanted to think about and what he wanted to do. Also Asmodeus didn't stay that long. The length of time he was inside Peter had increased but not by too much. Peter had never been gifted with any insight or clairvoyance so he was especially enjoying his connection to the 'other side'. He also found he could now travel in the astral plane. This meant that if Peter lay down on his bed and relaxed completely and focused on something or someone he found that after a short while he would be hovering over the scene watching from above. The more he did it, the more proficient he became and the more he realised how useful and powerful this gift was.

During the morning Peter had been trying Steve's home telephone number a few times and then he remembered Steve saying he wouldn't be at home. Peter went to his bedroom and lay down and concentrated his mind on Steve Conners. After quite a lot of practice Peter could now focus quite quickly and was soon looking down on Steve. Steve was sitting in an armchair reading but when Liz appeared in the room Peter naturally realised where Steve was, at Liz's flat still keeping an eye on her. After a while Peter returned to his body in the bedroom and he was so excited with his recent success with this, that he immediately rang Steve on his mobile. His adrenaline running Peter poured out his astral adventures finishing with his visit to Steve a few minutes earlier.

Steve could hardly contain his anger "Peter have you any idea what you are doing? To astral travel you have to leave your body completely, so for the period of time you are away your body is totally unprotected. I know what you are going to say, many religions have spiritual leaders who do this routinely but they have spent many years in training with a master, so they know how to do it with limited risk. Its like flying a plane, you have to be trained. You however, have no-one to keep an eye on your body when you astral travel and have no understanding of the dangers and how to lessen them. To make matters a hundred times worse, you have a resident demon who can and will step into you body at any time. Your absence will make it easy for it to take total possession." Peter replied "But Steve, Asmodeus steps into my body frequently but always steps out again." "In the names of all the Holy Gods Peter, don't you see the difference between the two situations? If Asmodeus steps in with you, you can at least resist him, if you aren't there he can totally possess your body and refuse to allow you back. You must never do that again and you need to get Asmodeus sent back to where he came from. Following your dedication ritual you now belong to the Satanic coven so you must talk to your Satanic High Priest, not to me. Can you imagine what your Satanic High Priest will say and do when he finds out you have been coming to me for advice. You are dedicated to him and Satan. You took an oath on your life and soul. Ask him to bind Asmodeus from you or better still send it back. You must not come round to Liz's flat or my house. You can ring me in an emergency but that is pointless if you don't take my advice. Remember your Satanic High Priest can and will watch your every move. I do wish you luck Peter, you are going to need it" and Steve hung up the phone.

Liz had walked into her lounge whilst Steve was on the phone and had sat down and was listening to Steve's end of the conversation.

"Steve, is Peter going to be alright?" Liz asked. "Not unless he changes tack" Steve said "he won't take advice. Peter keeps asking my advice but then totally ignores it. He spoke to me about joining the Satanic coven and I said no way, get out quickly. Peter joined and kept going. When Peter told me about dedication I warned him against it as strongly as possible. He promptly dedicated himself to Satan. He created a channel for a demon of lust and when he asked me I said to ask the High Priest to send it back. I don't think the High Priest can do that unless the person concerned demands it. As it is Peter seems to welcome the demon in his flat. Now Peter tells me he is experimenting with astral travel with no training or protection and a demon in residence. He needs to turn about or this will end badly." "What can we do Steve?" Liz asked. "Unfortunately nothing at all" Steve said "Peter has dedicated himself to Satan so I cannot and have no right to interfere. That is exactly what I tried to warn Peter against. To dedicate himself to Satan Peter had to forsake all other Gods, so no-one can help him except the Satanic High Priest and of course Satan himself."

During the afternoon Lauren rang Steve's mobile number and asked if he needed relieving. He said he was fine but they could do with some shopping. Checking over his shoulder to make sure Liz wasn't listening to his phone conversation, he said that Peter had become more unstable so he felt the risk had increased not decreased. Therefore he didn't even want to leave Liz on her own during daylight hours, at least not yet. He gave Lauren a list of shopping items over the phone and promised to pay her back when she arrived. "Thanks Lauren, really appreciate it" said Steve. Later that afternoon Lauren arrived with the shopping and when they were unpacking Liz spotted a bottle of white wine. "Now that is a good idea" and immediately put it in the fridge to cool. Lauren stayed for tea and they chatted light heartedly, avoiding subjects like Peter and demons.

Steve and Liz had a couple of glasses of wine with their steamed fish, peas and mash and watched a little television. Steve showered quite early in the evening and went off to bed. He tossed and turned for an hour and finally fell asleep. Suddenly there was a knock on his bedroom door and Steve was immediately wide awake. He thought it was the middle of the night, but it was actually only 11pm. He called out "Who is that?" Liz's voice answered "There are only two of us in this flat and it's not you knocking, so you only get one guess" "You sound very much awake, what's the problem?" replied Steve. The bedroom door opened a little and Liz's head appeared "That is the problem. I can't sleep. Will you come over to my room and talk to me?" said Liz. "Yes, that's fine. Give me a minute." Steve got up cleaned his teeth, not sure why, and checked his night clothes were decent and went next door.

***Duke Eligos is a Great Duke of Hell. The illustration
is from Dictionnaire Infernal by Collin de Plancy.
He is seen riding a winged horse the Steed of Abigor,
A name he is also called. The horse is said to be a minion
of Hell and a gift from Satan himself.

Liz had left the door ajar. As Steve went in he found Liz sitting up in bed. She smiled at him and patted on the bed next to her. It was a Queen-size double bed. Steve sat on the bed and asked what the problem was. Liz immediately started talking about Peter and the demon. She was very worried it was going to go wrong with Peter and then the demon would come back for her. Steve didn't want to lie but did his best to reassure her. Finally she asked Steve if he would sleep next to her and give her a cuddle. Steve just looked at her and went very quiet. He was trying to decide if he should tell her the truth about his feelings when Liz said "Is that so terrible Steve, that you want to run away?" The decision had now been made for him "No, not at all" Steve said "I think I had better tell you something. I find you very attractive, have done for some time. With our age difference I didn't want to make any advances. If I climbed in your bed for a cuddle I couldn't trust myself, so I think it's better I tuck you in and say good night". Liz broke into a big smile. "If that's the problem we don't have a problem. I have felt the same about you for months and when you protected me on Saturday night I just knew I was always going to feel that way about you. Go and get the wine bottle and two glasses and remember to come back." "I think I can cope with that" Steve said and he left her room. Three minutes later he returned holding the wine and two glasses. Liz had a big smile on her face. She had turned the lights down low and as he got to the bed she threw back the covers and Steve nearly dropped the wine. Liz was completely naked. Steve got the message. He put down the wine and glasses and climbed in with Liz. Liz decided Steve wasn't as old as he thought he was, when later she was able to arouse him for a third time in the early hours of the morning. They finally fell asleep at about 3 am and neither of them had thought about Peter or his demon even once.

It was gone 9am when Liz opened her eyes. She smiled and moved over and snuggled up to Steve. She was happier than she had been for a long time. She was very aware he was 26years older than her but he didn't look it or act it and she had already decided she would go for a few years of happiness rather than many years of disappointment. She knew Steve wouldn't let her down. Just knew it. And at any rate, she smiled at the thought, he's never going to leave her for a younger woman. When they were up, washed and dressed they sat down for breakfast and chatted over breakfast. They couldn't stop talking. Was this nervous overload or did they just get on that well? Liz told Steve what was on her mind "I was thinking when I woke up in bed Steve, I am happier than I have been for a long time, maybe ever. I know you are much older than me but you make me feel good, you make me feel safe. I would prefer whatever time I can have with you rather than a longer time with someone else." "Liz" Steve replied "I was thinking just when we least expect it love comes along. I have never felt like this with anyone. I have never talked like this with anyone, let alone the morning after. I really thought the chance of a good loving relationship had passed me by and then you come into my life. I am really happy as well." Liz replied with a very serious tone "What will happen when the problem with Peter and the demon is solved. Will you want to move out?" "Not unless you want me to" Steve replied. Liz had her elbows on the kitchen table and her hands wrapped around her tea mug. She smiled into her tea as though she had had a beautiful vision.

During Thursday Aleister had asked Dame Alice to phone the new starts and less experienced members of the coven for a teach-in on Saturday evening. There was no ritual on the Satanic calendar until Monday 2nd February which was Candlemass and no formal coven meeting had been arranged for the coming Saturday 10th January. So it was arranged that, Aleister and Dame Alice as the teachers were to be joined by George, Hecate, Sheila, Veronica and Peter. They were all told that there would be an informal chat in the lounge answering questions about the coven practices and workings and then some working in the circle, so they were to come with a question or two and bring their dominos.

Saturday 10th January started wet and windy and got no better as the day went on. In fact it got worse because in the evening, with the coming of darkness the cold made the wind really bitter. Nevertheless by 9pm all six of Aleister's guests had arrived safely and on time. The lounge in the Pinnacle was warm and comforting. The heating had been turned up and they were all given a warm mulled wine as they entered. Castor had arranged seven comfortable armchairs in a circle with a coffee table in the centre on which stood a jug of hot mulled wine for top ups. The illuminated head of the Goat of Mendes looked down on the circle. After handing over their hats, scarves and coats to Castor, the guests all gladly took a glass of warm wine and made themselves comfortable.

After welcoming all of them to his home Aleister explained the plan for the evening. He would allow a few questions about the occult, the coven, the rituals or workings. They would then go to the circle and practice a routine 'coning'. "Right Sheila what is your question?" Aleister asked. "High Priest, can you please explain what coning is" said Sheila. "Sheila I did talk about coning quite recently but I don't think you were there and tonight will be your first time in the circle, so it's a fair question. This practice was made famous by our Patron Demoness Astaroth. The circle of members hold hands and they all focus on the centre of the floor projecting their energies to that point. After a while they move the centre of concentration of the energies upward a few feet. They continue to do this until that centre is above their heads. If they have been successful they will have a cone shaped energy force. The forces of the energies are starting at the circle, being the base of the cone and the point at the top becomes the peak of energy concentration. As I said that cone shape of energy was pioneered by Astaroth and she became known for this cone. This black cone became synonymous with Astaroth, to the extent that ignorant people believed it was the hats her circle members wore, not the power they created. Hence the black cone became known ever since as the witches' hat.

Right, what is your question Veronica?" Aleister asked. "Shortly after I joined this coven High Priest, we had a Halloween party. It was great, lots of food and drink and sex but I don't actually know what Halloween is. Can you please tell me?" Veronica asked. "Yes of course, but to answer your question I need to explain some religious history. We are going back over two thousand years before Christianity. The British people were farmers. Their lives revolved around growing and harvesting crops to survive. They worshipped the Pagan Gods especially Eostra the Goddess of fertility because whether their crops fertilised or their animals successfully bred dictated their survival. Everything they did was based upon the cycle of life and the seasons. Their calendar year was therefore divided into the four seasons and then again for the equinoxes making eight segments. Their new year was 31st October called Sam Hein (pronounced sow-enn).

As they were farmers they had their own land so when grandma died she was buried on their land. On the night of 31st October they celebrated Sam Hein by making a circle of candles around their family graves and they sat in the circle and talked to their parents and grand parents. As it was new year they told their ancestors what they had done that year and what they planned for the future. The children were all included as well, it was not grotesque, it was a happy occasion.

When the Romans came to Britain they brought their Christianity with them and they took over all the old festivals including Sam Hein. They called 1ˢᵗ November All Saints Day and 31ˢᵗ October then became All Hallows Eve. Some Roman Catholics still practice All Hallows Eve and in Italy especially, the Priests walk around the grave yards swinging incense and sprinkling Holy water on the graves and blessing the dead.

In the middle ages when Christians were encouraged to persecute Pagans they told people that on All Hallows Eve the Pagans got the dead to rise up out of their graves and painted grotesque images of their celebration. This celebration then became known as Halloween not All Hallows Eve. Like all the old festivals, such as Yuletide and Easter, most of the people who celebrate them have no idea what they represent. The result of these historical events is that nowadays on the night of 31ˢᵗ October some Roman Catholics follow their Priest around the cemetery whilst they bless the dead, some Christians celebrate All Hallows Eve in a church and Pagans still celebrate Sam Hein as New Year by talking to their ancestors. We Satanists however were in a privileged position as we had no real commitment to 31ˢᵗ October, as New Year or as All Hallows Eve. However, the Pagans have been talking to their ancestors on that night for hundreds of years, and in so doing have created a window to the other-side. We as Satanists have found that on the night of 31ˢᵗ October it is easier to break the bonds of the doors to the 'other-side'. This has now become a norm for Satanic covens, to the extent that Halloween is now one of our two most important celebrations. This celebration for Satanists now has a history of blood rituals and sexual association with demons which can provide us with many gifts and powers. Serious rituals of this nature are restricted to initiates in the circle but other members are allowed a party which you were naturally invited to. I will allow you one further question."

Hecate asked "Can I ask a question High Priest?" "Of course, go ahead Hecate" Aleister replied. "I have heard many times about Friday 13ᵗʰ being unlucky for some. Is that true? Where does it come from?" "It comes from the history of the Knights Templars" Aleister replied. "Shortly after the First Crusade in 1120 Hugues de Payens, a French aristocrat brought together eight relatives who were knights and formed the order. Their objective was to protect pilgrims on their journey to Holy Places. King Baldwin ll of Jerusalem gave them headquarters on the Temple Mount. The Templars headquarters were in the Aqsa Mosque which stood on the site of Solomon's Temple. The Knights then used this association in their name: Pauperes commilitones Christi Templique Solomonici which means 'the poor soldiers of Christ and of the Temple of Solomon'. This was shortened to Knights Templars.

New members to the order of the Knights Templars had to make vows of obedience, chastity and poverty and pass all their wealth to the brotherhood. Pope Innocent II made an order 'Omne Datum Optimum' which stated that the Knights Templars could travel through any countries and were subject to no rules other than the Pope's. The Knights Templars were few in numbers but would join other armies and would make what became known as a squadron charge. On heavily armed horses they would make a very tight formation and charge the enemies front ranks with such ferocity that they would break a hole in the enemies lines and help win the battle. However by the late 13th century King Philip of France had started to mistrust the Knights Templars as they had declared their desire for their own state in Languedoc in South Eastern France. The Templars were no longer fighting in the Holy Land so their army had no battle to fight. They had the Pope's authority to travel where they liked and they paid no taxes plus King Philip had inherited an empty purse from his father and had debts to the Knights Templar. On Friday 13th October 1307, at dawn, scores of Knights Templars in France were arrested simultaneously, by authority of King Philip of France. They were tortured until they admitted heresy and then put to death. Friday 13th has ever since been a date of foreboding.

Hecate, you will better understand the significance and importance of the Temple of Solomon as you progress in the coven. Solomon was a very great sorcerer as was evidenced in the Key of Solomon, in the 14th century, The Clavicle of Solomon in 1572 and the Greater Key of Solomon of 1889, all of which had been translated to Latin. We will study these at a much later date." Aleister then turned and looked at them all. "We must now move on to our physical lesson. Please bring your dominos and follow Dame Alice and me." They followed Aleister and Alice as they walked out of the lounge into the entrance hall. They walked down the full length of the corridor and up the stairs coming into the bathrooms. "Please disrobe and carry your domino with you" Dame Alice said. "Normally we all thoroughly shower first to ensure we are completely clean when we enter the circle. However we are not preparing a protective circle this time, so we will not be calling the corners, inviting the elementals, demons or Gods, or setting up the altar. This session is to get you familiar with stepping into the circle, slipping into your domino and the physical routine of creating a cone of power. You are unlikely to achieve this time but we want you to have the feel of the routine, hence the dominos.

Right follow the lead of the High Priest, myself, George and Hecate." The four of them stepped into the bathroom, removed their clothes and stepped back out skyclad, with their gowns or dominos over their arms. They opened the door to the Temple and walked through. The High Priest and Priestess slid their gowns on as they got to the circle and stepped inside. George and Hecate waited a few moments for the others to catch up and they all slid on their dominos and stepped into the circle. Sheila, Veronica and Peter had looked a little uncomfortable but soon settled once they had their dominos on and were in the circle. Alice moved them deeper into the circle away from the circle edge. Normally there would be thirteen members around the edge of the circle but as there was seven they had to make a much smaller circle. They were told to face inwards and hold hands. They then had to stand with their legs apart so that their feet touched the person's feet on each side of them. They were told to pull up their hoods because it helps novices avoid distractions and concentrates the eyes and thoughts to the area ahead. They started off concentrating their energy on the centre of the floor and slowly over a half hour period they moved upwards towards the ceiling.

Later back in the comfortable seats of the lounge Aleister listened to comments he had heard a hundred times before. Novices were always surprised how tired they were afterwards and yet they had been projecting their energy away from their body to a central place. Aleister did feel the energy so although not impressive at this stage, they were getting the idea. Aleister could see they were all getting tired. He told Hecate that he would contact her about Candlemass and with Alice he escorted them to the front door. After the five new members left Aleister looked at Alice and said how pleased he was that Peter did not have anything with him. They hoped that that would continue without their intervention.

CHAPTER 14

Gwendoline's Preparation

Sunday 11th January dawned cold, wet and windy, like the day before. Liz climbed out of bed and after looking out the window and seeing the state of the weather, she turned her heating up and promptly returned to bed and snuggled up to Steve. Liz felt that they were like an old married couple in that they had fused together so easily. She didn't just mean sexually, although that was really good but in every way. Their routines, likes and dislikes had melted together like they were meant to be. She was very happy. Steve groaned and moved in the bed. Liz rolled over onto her left side and her right hand slid under the bedclothes and she started to arouse him. Steve's groan changed to more like a purr. 'Wasn't Sunday morning invented for sleeping in and having sex? I am sure it must be a rule written down somewhere' Liz thought. Any way who the Hell wants to go outside in this weather. 'If I make him happy, maybe he'll make me breakfast in bed' she thought.

Steve was happy but he didn't make her breakfast in bed. However he did do a cooked breakfast for them both and they chatted over the kitchen table, both content. Liz said "You have a wonderful relationship between your coven members and yourself. They all look up to you and totally trust you. For that reason alone I would love to become part of your coven." Steve replied "That's not really good enough reason to join a coven. You join a coven because you have similar religious beliefs. I say similar, not the same, because every Pagan has different beliefs but they all believe in the same principles." "What principles are you talking about?" asked Liz. Steve replied "All Pagans believe there is more than one God. They believe in a Goddess who rules Nature upon the Earth and the many spirits that surround us. Life is reliant upon fertility and fertility is reliant upon the female to produce and foster growth. How can there not be a feminine Goddess? Pagans believe in protecting nature, the sanctity of life, the right and freedom to serve and worship their own choice of God and Goddess. If you walked around our circle and asked the members which Gods and Goddesses do they worship, you will find them saying different names. The truth is their names don't change because we give them different names. The names don't matter; they are probably the same Gods whether they have Egyptian, Greek, Roman, Nordic or Celtic names.

Pagans don't believe us humans own the world, Pagans believe the world owns us and we have a duty to protect and nurture it and we worship all living things. We are sometimes called tree huggers because Pagans will hug or even worship a tree. In return for our devotion to the true Gods and Goddesses and to the Earth we are given gifts and some of us are given powers. These gifts and powers are not for our own betterment but to enable us to achieve our protective goals. That may include protecting our own, our coven members and families." "As you did a week ago, on that Saturday night" Liz said and continued "So what do Pagans believe about Jesus?" "Most Pagans do not believe he is a Son of God but we do honour him as a great prophet. The point is that Jesus may have been a great teacher and leader but he was teaching and leading the people in the Middle East and his understandings and principles were therefore designed and intended for those nations.

Christianity was brought here by our invaders and was imposed upon us for political reasons to enable them to rule and control us. This Eastern religion was alien to us and we should have rejected it. However Pagans believe, literally, in live and let live, and those who follow Jesus have our blessing to do so. Please remember we are the good guys. The Christians persecuted and burnt us alive, not the other way around. Yet we bare no hatred for them or their beliefs. I personally have gone into Christian churches many times; sometimes invited by enlightened leaders to talk to their brethren and sometimes because a Christian friend is having a marriage or baptism."

Liz then asked "There appears to be many common areas in Paganism and Satanism Steve. Can you explain the main differences between them." "Yes of course Liz" Steve said "Firstly I have to say that most Pagans do not believe in Satan as a deity. Satan was created by and is part of Christianity, one of their fallen angels. We believe that the evil comes from men's hearts and not some celestial being. However this evil can be born, nurtured and grown from our actions, our experiences and what we are exposed to in life. Mixing and practising with Satanists will without doubt, propagate that very evil. However, historically most religions are connected. That is why Roman Catholic Priests or Orthodox Greek Priests or Pagan Priests act in a very similar way. Our rituals are nearly identical. We have ceremonial gowns, altars, candles, ring bells, swing incense containers, sprinkle salt and Holy Water. The Satanists do the same. The difference is in the religion's intentions. We foster love and understanding whereas Satanists foster hate and dominance. Do not look at a religion's actions but at its results. Do they engender love and happiness or lust and hatred? Does the religion teach and encourage the protection of life or does it engender hatred to kill those that disagree with its teachings? The Bible said 'Ye shall know them by their fruits' Matthew Chapter 7 verse 16."

"So why are all the rituals of different faiths so similar?" Liz asked. Steve replied "It is the principle of Pavlov's dog. Simple psychology known as conditioned response. You do something and it works, so you do it again and build upon it. By this means spiritual rituals have been formed that are echoed by many different religions and over many many years spiritual gifts have been discovered and magick learnt. Modern man and woman have moved away from nature and are no longer sensitive to the needs and vibrations of nature. But principles were learnt and understood many years ago and sometimes recorded; The Key of Solomon and The Great Grimoire of Pope Honorius III, to name just two. The Egyptians, Jews, Greeks, Romans and Celts have been very thorough in recording their spiritual successes with rituals. It could therefore be argued whatever the religion we may all be tapping into the same power." "I don't understand that Steve" Liz said "some religions are wonderfully Holy like Buddhism and some disgustingly evil like Satanism. How can they be feeding from the same trough?" "Let me explain it another way" said Steve. "We need to think of all spiritual forces as power just like electricity. The forefathers and leaders of many different religions have discovered these powers of nature and used ritual magick to tap into them. Mostly they have used this power for good, used this electricity to cook meals for starving people, or to bring light to the darkness. But you can also use electricity to deliberately electrocute someone. An athame is a magickal ritual knife that can be used to generate power, but think for a moment of a normal kitchen knife. You can use a knife to prepare a meal or carve a beautiful sculpture but you can also kill with it. The principle is the same with an athame. I like to think that a Pagan Priest is holding the athame to generate power to heal someone or bring confidence into someone's life. A Satanic Priest maybe holding an athame to sacrifice chickens, to drink their blood, as part of a spell to curse someone. We live in the same world, we are part of the same nature, we tap into the same power. It is not the power but what you do with it that makes the difference. Remember ye shall know them by their fruits."

"Everything" Liz said "makes me want to join your coven. I love you but I also trust and respect you. I want to be with you. I want to support you. I want to help you with your work." "Once we have resolved this problem with Peter and his resident demon" Steve replied "and we know you are not going to be targeted by the demon, there is no reason whatsoever that we can't bring you into the coven. Look Liz, I am not prepared to leave you alone here for one moment, even in the daytime to get food until we have resolved this problem. However I was thinking that if this situation with Peter does drag on I might ask you if our coven could meet here in your lounge. It would also mean you could meet everyone and see how you feel. How does that sound?" As Liz immediately gave him a hug and a kiss, he took that as a yes.

On the same day, Sunday 11th, during the afternoon, Tamsin brought her niece Gwendoline around to Hecate's small country cottage in Wychamton, near Seaford. Tamsin had explained to Gwendoline that a close friend was unwell and she needed to spend time with her, however her best friend Hecate had agreed to look after her. Tamsin helped Gwendoline pack everything she had into her two small suitcases. She explained to her that her friend was very ill and she would be at least three weeks away but it could be longer.

When Tamsin and Gwendoline arrived at the cottage, Hecate took Gwendoline and her two cases upstairs to a small bedroom that she had prepared for her. Hecate had made it very pretty and feminine with a bedspread and pillows decorated with pink poppies together with delicate lace on the bedside cabinets. Hecate showed Gwendoline the chest of draws and wardrobe and told her to unpack. "Unpack all your things and put them away to suit yourself. You can take your time, there is no rush. Get to know your new room and settle in. Come downstairs when you are ready.

Tamsin waited in the lounge while Hecate put the kettle on and called out from the kitchen as to how Tamsin liked her tea. When Hecate came into the lounge they both settled in easy chairs and Hecate served the tea. The two ladies were completed different in many ways. Whilst Tamsin was forty eight years of age, short and very overweight and had a strong Ulster accent, Hecate was only twenty five years of age, tall, shapely, beautiful and spoke as though she had been brought up by private education. The truth was that Hecate had come from a working class family but she had her sights firmly set on wealth and power. The accent was because she worked as a legal secretary and focused on 'fitting in' with her employers and the wealthy customers. "Tell me" Hecate said "where does the name Tamsin come from?" "Aleister named me after Tamsin Blight a nineteenth century Cornish witch who died in 1856" Tamsin replied. "Ah, I think I remember now" Hecate said "wasn't she the witch who practiced as a shaman summoning and talking to spirits. She specialised in treating and healing cattle and was therefore very popular with the farmers." "Exactly right" Tamsin said.

*** The 'Blocksbergs Verrichtung' of 1668 by
Johannes Praetorius, has an illustration supposedly
showing traditional medieval Satanic rituals.

"Can I suggest" Hecate said "that while Gwendoline is upstairs
we take the opportunity to discuss Gwendoline?" "Yes of course,
we must" Tamsin replied. "Right," Hecate said "I am going to tell
you my understanding of what is going to happen and what I need
to do and you must correct me as necessary. This preparation is for
the celebration of Candlemass which we are going to celebrate on
2nd February. I got Aleister's permission and looked in our Book of
Shadows. It states that Candlemass (the Pagan's call it Imbolc) should
really be celebrated when the sun is at fifteen degrees of Aquarius, that
is midway between the Winter Solstice and the Spring Equinox. That
means the special alignment gives the night greater power for magickal
workings. Traditionally Satanic covens sacrifice a virgin on this night.
Contrary to public opinion this is by sexual penetration, that is the
virginity is sacrificed, not the girl. This confers from Satan further
powers on the coven. Aleister agreed that the celebration should be

midway between Winter Solstice and Spring Equinox because these seasonal quarters are known as Sabbats and are excellent times for spells. This Sabbat is about Fire, it is a fire Celebration. Aleister said he will tell us more on the night.

I understand from Dame Alice, Gwendoline is a virgin and has been brought up by nuns in a nunnery. This makes her very special and perfect for our needs. Alice said that to desecrate her will bring great favour and power from our Lord Satan. Alice tells me Gwendoline is given a glass of brandy every night and this has now been increased to a full measure. I will tell Gwendoline she needs a little help to sleep and start giving her a small dose of midazolam from tonight so that by the 2nd February she will be accustomed to the medication and we will be able to give her a strong enough dose to anaesthetize her." Tamsin, with concern in her voice said "Midazolam is a very strong drug Hecate, where will you get it and how do you know how much to give her?" Hecate replied "As you have been with the coven for over 5 years now, Dame Alice said you rarely need her support and has now become my mentor since my initiation. Alice is guiding me down this path. She gave me the midazolam, together with a small measure cup. The midazolam is 2mg in a ml so I am to give Gwendoline only 2 mls a night at bedtime. We will give her 10 mgs on the night and maybe a further 10 mgs if necessary. Alice tells me midazolam also has an amnesiac effect, so Gwendoline won't be able to remember what happened on the night, which of course is very useful as far as the coven is concerned. However midazolam is very short acting so the effect doesn't last that long. We will have to be very careful with timing Gwendoline's drink and medication on the night.

Ah, I think I hear Gwendoline coming down the stairs. Is there anything I have said Tamsin, that you disagree with or I have got wrong?" "No not at all, Hecate. You have done your homework. Very impressive I must say." As Tamsin said this, Gwendoline came into the lounge. "I have to leave now Gwendoline" Tamsin said. "You are in safe hands with Hecate. Any problems, talk to her." Tamsin took her cup and saucer back to the kitchen and left through the front door. Hecate then showed Gwendoline around the rest of the cottage. She made sure Gwendoline knew which facecloths and towels to use and where the kettle, microwave, fridge, tea and coffee were. She also showed her how to work the TV system and where she could play her own CDs. Hecate thought Gwendoline was gentle and co-operative and wouldn't be a problem.

Over the next two weeks Lauren had twice turned up at Liz's flat with bags of groceries. In Steve's absence Lauren had called a meeting of the coven and they were all concerned about Steve and Liz's food and finances. Both Steve and Liz were self employed and neither of them had worked since before Yuletide (Christmas). Luckily Steve's house was bought and paid for but he must still be getting bills on his door mat he can't pay. The coven members decided they can at least make sure the two of them don't starve. There was comments like 'you can't live on love alone' so their new relationship was common knowledge! They had a whip round and raised some money and Lauren went to the supermarket.

On Monday 26th January, the phone at Liz's flat rang during the morning. Liz picked it up and when she said "Oh, Hi Peter, how are you?" Steve shot across the lounge and snatched the phone from Liz. Liz glared at Steve but didn't do anything, just listened to what Steve said. Steve was telling Peter that if he is having problems with Asmodeus he needs to go and see the Satanic High Priest immediately. "Peter we love you dearly but you are your own worst enemy. I told you not to join that coven. I told you not to go through with the dedication ritual. You ring me for advice but don't act on my advice. From what you told me last time your Satanic High Priest knows this demon and he knows how to send it back. Don't wait any longer. If the demon is entering you and you are beginning to have difficulty getting it to leave you, you must act immediately. I hate to say this but you mustn't speak to Liz, not even on the phone, you know the demon was interested in her and you will create a channel for it to come back to her. Go and see the Satanic High Priest. You can ring us when he has sent the demon back to where it came from, not before. I am going to hang up now."

As Steve put the phone down he looked at Liz "I'm sorry about that Liz. Didn't mean to be rude to you but you mustn't talk to Peter, not even on the phone. As it turns out Peter is having problems with this demon. If the demon is inside him when he speaks to you a channel is created which the demon can use to get to you. You heard what I said to him. Once Peter has gone to the Satanic High Priest and got him to send the demon back, we can see and talk to Peter. I will then see if it is possible to cancel Peter's dedication oaths to Satan but I can't even think about that unless Peter wants that and specifically requests it." "I thought" Liz said "that the dedication rite is permanent and cannot be reversed." "That is correct or should I say that is what we are always told. However any oath can be withdrawn or overturned but there is usually penalties. When Peter took his oath of dedication to Satan, at the end of the oath, he would have had to say that should he break this oath then there will be consequences, which he then signed in his own blood. He will have a copy of the oath he signed and I would need to see it to look at those consequences before I could advise him. Satanic consequences are likely to be bad. It's a question of whether he is prepared to accept those consequences or if I can protect him from them. It would have been so much better if he had listened and not done the dedication ritual."

CHAPTER 15

The Feast of Fire

The morning of 2nd February, arrived with a bright clear sky but very cold. A heavy frost lay across the lawns of the Pinnacle. As Castor walked outside he found Aleister in his bedroom robe with his usual cup of coffee, looking at the frost and in deep thought. "Castor" Aleister said "Christians call this day Candlemass but most Pagans call it Imbolc. The word Pagan comes from the Latin 'pagus' meaning country and 'pagani' meaning those who live in the country. Pagans are sometimes called heathen, often meant as a form of insult. However Heathen comes from old English 'hoeben' meaning heath, hence heathen is a heath dweller, again someone from the country. Their celebration Imbolc (pronounced immolk) means lambs' milk. The name of the Pagan celebration comes from the fact that Pagans were country dwellers and therefore farming folk and early February was the time for lambing which meant the ewes were with milk. It was also the time of snow drops blooming and when the farmers saw the snow drops in bloom, all the little drops of white across the fields, it made them think of lambs' milk. Whereas the name Candlemass celebration actually got its name from another ancient festival, long before Christianity. The name was originally the Feast of Lights or the Feast of Fire and it celebrated the increase strength of the sun as winter gave way to spring. It marks the midpoint between the shortest day of the year and the spring equinox."

Castor stood looking at Aleister as though waiting. "You want your instructions for preparation for tonight don't you?" Aleister said. Castor nodded. "We will celebrate indoors. As I said this is a Feast of Lights so apart from the four coloured candles marking the corners I want thirty two black candles, around the circle, that is eight candles in each quarter. In the centre I want the small cauldron with one of the eight inch wide black candles inside it. Tell the kitchen staff we want enough food and drink for twenty revellers, I actually make the number eighteen but lets be on the generous side. There must be a table in the entrance hall with an adequate selection of glasses of our special port and sherry with the aphrodisiac added. You need to welcome everyone with a drink excepting Dame Alice, Gwendoline and Sheila. The rest of the drink, a generous selection of wines, spirits and mixers, is to be available in the lounge from eight thirty and the food is to be laid out at eleven, in time for our return to the lounge. It can be mainly a cold buffet as we haven't been outside, but it should traditionally include crepes and pancakes. Their rounded shapes and golden colour are symbolic of the returning sun which is very relevant with this celebration. Make sure the heating in the Temple is high, we will be skyclad. Also make sure the Goat of Mendes mask and the singing bowl and mallet are on the altar. Any queries come and see me." Castor nodded and walked back inside. Aleister spent the morning making sure the kitchen staff had enough supplies and checking that the Temple and circle were cleaned and ready. He later went to his rooms and lay down for a rest. Early evening he spent in meditation and prayer, he needed to be sure he could achieve penetration and convey the gifts he had chosen.

At 8 o'clock in the evening Dame Alice was the first to arrive. She came in and without touching the drinks in the entrance hall she entered the lounge and sat down opposite Aleister. "You wanted to discuss the gifts High Priest?" Alice said. "Yes" Aleister replied. "I have chosen Tamsin and Margaret to receive the gift of scrying and George to receive hypnotism and the evil eye. They have all earned some reward. Are you in agreement with that?" "Yes High Priest, total agreement." "Good. I will tell them in the circle. Now as you know Sheila is not well and has asked for healing. I am going to ask Margaret to take Sheila to the bathrooms when she arrives. I will also ask Margaret to offer Sheila a sedative drink as she hasn't been initiated yet and isn't used to skyclad. I see Hecate has just arrived with Gwendoline. Can I leave you to offer Hecate a drink if she wants one and take them both through to the bathrooms. Gwendoline is to have 10 mgs of medication at 9.30 if that isn't enough she can have the other 10 mgs at 10 pm. Remind Hecate to use a lubricator on Gwendoline to assist my entry. When Gwendoline is deeply asleep, Hecate is to come into the Temple and nod to me. Hecate will join the circle and Castor will carry Gwendoline to the edge of the circle. I'll see you in the circle." Dame Alice went over to Hecate and Gwendoline, whilst Aleister went to talk to Margaret about Sheila.

At 9pm fifteen coven members started, one by one, to step through the door from the bathrooms into the Temple, leaving only Sheila, Hecate and Gwendoline behind. Castor stood in the Temple by the door awaiting further instructions. The Temple was as warm as the bathrooms, which was good, as apart from Castor they were all skyclad. As each member stepped into the Temple their eyes widened with the amazing sight. All the lights in the temple were off except two spot lights. One spotlight was aimed at the Goat of Mendes image on the wall above the altar and the other spotlight illuminated the Dark Circle on the ceiling. However the Temple wasn't dark, it was in fact a mass of sparkling and dancing candle flames. There were no less than thirty six large candles around the edge of the circle and two further candles on the altar and finally a huge black candle standing in the cauldron in the centre of the circle. Between them they produced a breathtaking display of flickering flames, reflecting on the walls and ceiling, with dancing lights and shadows. It really was Candlemass. These coven members were all seasoned members and walked to the circle skyclad but without any discomfort. They had all seen each-other many times and were more focused on the ritual than each-other.

When they had all entered the circle, taking care not to burn themselves, they took their designated places around the perimeter and Aleister blessed the water and sprinkled it around the perimeter and then did the same with the salt. They then started calling the corners, the Kings of Hell, to hear them, to join them. The High Priest then called upon Astaroth to join them and then called upon the Almighty and Ineffable God Satan the one true original God, and then cried at the top of his voice 'Hail Satan'. All the candles flickered and dimmed for a second or two. They all thought the candles were going to go out, but the flames recovered and the brightness returned. It was a sign that the Lord Satan had heard their cry and was aware of them.

Aleister then called across to Castor to bring Sheila across to the circle. Castor disappeared inside the bathroom door and then quickly emerged with Sheila. Sheila was definitely mesmerised by all the lights when she came into the Temple but quickly recovered herself. Castor walked Sheila over to the circle and was obviously instructing her as they came across. At the edge of the circle Castor left her and turned back to the bathrooms. Aleister told Sheila to step into the circle but to be careful with all the burning candles. Aleister held out his hand and guided Sheila to the centre, next to the cauldron. He asked her to kneel and walked around behind her. He placed his hands on her head and looked towards Dame Alice who went over and collected the singing bowl from the altar. The members all moved inwards slightly until they could all hold hands. Then they spread their legs so their feet touched each-other. There was now a circular wall of the coven all touching each-others hands and feet. As they settled in position Dame Alice started running the mallet around the singing bowl and the coven members started to "Ummm" together. Then they started to sway in unison. They were staring and concentrating on Sheila and after a while the power in the circle was tangible. Slowly, very slowly they moved their concentration upwards building a cone of power around Sheila. After about forty to fifty minutes Aleister brought his hands down to Sheila's elbows and gently raised her to her feet but she wasn't actually standing on the floor. There was a noticeable gap of about three inches between her feet and the floor. For a few minutes Sheila was weightless, totally supported by the cone of power. Aleister nodded to Dame Alice and she started to slow the speed of the singing bowl. The members also started to bring their concentration back downwards to the ground. It must have been about an hour after it started and they all realised Sheila was again supporting her own weight. Sheila looked radiant but dazed. Once she was fully recovered, Aleister told her to return to the bathrooms and shower and dress. "You are free to return home and Dame Alice will check on you tomorrow."

Once Sheila had left the Temple Aleister raised his voice and addressed them all. "We are gathered here tonight to make sacrifice of the virginity of a young innocent Christian girl to our Lord and Master Satan. If our sacrifice is accepted by Satan and should it please him we will confer spiritual gifts from Satan to three of our members." Aleister noticed how the members quickly glanced at each-other, each wondering who were to be the privileged members. As Aleister said this, the door from the bathrooms opened and Hecate appeared. When Aleister looked at her she smiled and nodded. Aleister also nodded and then called to Hecate for Castor to bring the sacrifice. Hecate disappeared into the bathrooms and reappeared skyclad three minutes later, followed by Castor, who was dressed, carrying Gwendoline as though she was a large rag doll. Hecate walked to the circle and when Aleister nodded, stepped inside. Then when Castor stood at the perimeter he passed Gwendoline over to Aleister, Dame Alice and Hecate. The three of them turned and laid Gwendoline on her back, lengthwise on the altar. The High Priest picked up the mask of the Goat of Mendes and put it on. This was to signify the sacrifice was being taken by Satan. Aleister climbed on the altar, aroused himself and quickly entered the girl. For a moment it looked as though she was waking up but Aleister managed to finish before she did wake. Aleister rose to his knees on the altar over the girl, raised his hands in the air and cried "Accept this sacrifice in your honour Almighty Satan" and they all joined in when he cried 'Hail Satan' and again the candle flames flickered and threatened to extinguish. The brightness returned almost immediately and Aleister, after removing his mask, helped Dame Alice and Hecate lift up Gwendoline and pass her back to Castor who had been waiting patiently. They obviously wanted to get Gwendoline back in the bathrooms before she woke up.

"I want to take this opportunity" Aleister said "of rewarding dedicated members by conferring spiritual gifts from Satan. I believe that Satan has signalled his approval of our sacrifice by the use of the candles, very appropriate on Candlemass. I therefore believe he will honour the gifts that we propose.

Firstly is George. We named him after George Pickingill, a significant figure in Paganism. George Pickingill was born in Essex and was credited with forming nine covens and reforming witchcraft.

He was part of the Hermetic Order of the Golden Dawn but was later thrown out due to his dedication to Satan. Our George has been very supportive with the selection of the site for the Pinnacle which has been very successful. We confer on him the gift of hypnotism and the evil eye. As he learns and practises he will find he will be able to control other people when it is to his advantage and also to destroy certain people who oppose or abuse him. Satan blesses you." "Hail Satan" they all cried.

"Secondly is Tamsin. We named her after Tamsin Blight a nineteenth century witch from Cornwall. She was known as the 'White Witch of Helstone' and one of the greatest conjurors of Britain. She could summon and talk to spirits and provided herbal cures for sick cattle which made her very popular with the farmers. Tamsin Blight died in 1856. Our Tamsin has been very instrumental in obtaining and grooming a sacrifice for this ritual. She has been an initiated member for over five years now and we wish to show our approval. We confer on her the gift of scrying. Without the risks of astral travel, after practise, you will be able to oversee anybody and in any place. This is a powerful weapon. I use it all the time. You will have to practise with different mediums, for example water, mirror, or crystal, to establish which works best for you. Satan blesses you." "Hail Satan" they all cried.

"Last but certainly not least is Margaret. We named her after Margaret Murray who was born in Calcutta, India in 1863. She was an expert Egyptologist who worked with the famous Sir William Flinders Petrie in Palestine and Egypt, at the end of the nineteenth century. She also became an expert on pagan culture and was the author of 'The God of Witches' and 'The Witch Cult of Western Europe'. She was 100 years old when she died in 1963. Our Margaret has been with this coven and a member of the circle for over ten years now. She has especially been a wonderful support for new initiates and we wish to thank her loyalty to Satan. We also confer on her the gift of scrying. It is a wonderful skill, can be very advantageous and can be achieved at any place or time. Satan blesses you." "Hail Satan" they all cried.

"Before we close this ritual and open this circle I want to do something that is very traditional with this celebration. This celebration was originally called the Feast of Flames or the Feast of Fire. It celebrates the increasing strength of the sun as spring approaches. We are sometimes given insight by looking into the central flames in the circle. This is called Pyromancy. We use the flames on this special night to divine the future. We interpret the shapes, directions and intensity of the flames and any images that are formed by them. As he said that Aleister squatted down in front of the great candle in the cauldron and concentrated on the candle's flame. Suddenly Aleister shook his head and got up quickly. "No" he said "it isn't working tonight. Let us call the corners and open the circle." Turning to the circle members he said "I am sure you will join George, Tamsin and Margaret in celebration and take advantage of all the food and drink in the lounge." Dame Alice who knew Aleister very well, knew something was wrong but this wasn't the time. She would ask him later when their guests had left or gone to bed.

Once the circle was open they all made their way to the bathrooms and there was much joy and laughter as they showered and dressed. They then very happily made their way down to the lounge and those staying for the night took great delight in consuming large quantities of food and wine. The aphrodisiac must have been working well as several members were already being very tactile in the lounge and went off to the same room. Gwendoline had long since woken up and Hecate had taken her back to her cottage some time ago. Tamsin would no doubt collect Gwendoline the next day. As the guests either left the house or made their way up to their rooms Dame Alice quietly approached Aleister. She could see he was still upset about something but was keeping it hidden, at least from everyone except Alice." Are you sleeping in your own room tonight Aleister? I see you are upset and I wondered if you wanted company to discuss it?" Aleister thought about it and then nodded. "I would like company and I would appreciate someone I can talk to about my thoughts and worries. Yes, please join me."

Later after Aleister had showered and changed for bed he poured himself a double scotch, pumped up the pillows and sat in bed thinking. Shortly afterwards, Alice knocked and came in. As usual she was dressed in a long but beautiful gown. She did exactly the same as Aleister, pumping up the pillows on the other side of the bed so she could sit up but after removing her dressing gown, she chose a double brandy. "I appreciate your company and would value it all night. I just want warm company, nothing against Rachel but tonight I need intellect as well, especially you." Alice knew there was no sexual intention with Aleister. He didn't really like sexual intercourse and Rachel was well practised in satisfying his sexual needs. No, Aleister was worried, which is very unusual for him. She knew something serious had happened but would let Aleister get round to it, in his own time.

As it was, it didn't take him very long. He discussed the ritual that night and how everything went smoothly but then became more stressed when he started talking about Sheila. "Tell me if I'm wrong Alice, but I felt the cone of power was very successful. It lifted Sheila off the ground which is usually the indicator that the power is getting through. Also I felt that Sheila was radiating that power afterwards." "You are right Aleister. So what has upset you?" Alice asked. "When I crouched down for the pyromancy" Aleister said "I saw a shape that could have only been a ghost, a spirit, a soul come up from the flames and go upwards in the smoke. It was very clear. The message was definitely intended for me." "And you think that refers to Sheila?" "Without any doubt, Sheila is terminally ill, her doctors have told her so. The whole point of members joining our coven and dedicating themselves to Satan is that we can change their lives for the better. We can prolong youth, create wealth and power, make people popular who were previously despised and of course heal their sickness. If Sheila dies it will truly damage the faith the members have in this coven and that will affect their dedication and loyalty." "Aleister, I honestly think you are jumping to conclusions too quickly. The message may be symbolic or a warning, not foretelling an event at all. You are very tired and stressed. Lie down and sleep. I will stay with you. In the morning we will look in the waters of the font and see what they have to say. They may show us what message is meant. Think about it, Satan will not allow what you fear. Trust him."

CHAPTER 16

The Consequences

It was Tuesday 3rd February, the day after Candlemass. Peter was not working; he had the day off as he had to work next Saturday. Peter had developed a real problem with his demon. Last week Asmodeus wasn't really a problem, he would come and go but it wasn't dominating him. That had changed. Now Asmodeus was either in him or with him permanently. It meant that Peter wasn't himself, as they say. He had loads of confidence and a massive libido and when Asmodeus was inside him all the ladies appeared naked. Peter knew it wasn't real just a mental game Asmodeus played with him. It was fun but could be very awkward as well. Such as, at his interview this morning. He had previously applied for a job at a large well established estate agency in Eastbourne. He quite enjoyed working at the café but the money was basic so he never had any spare cash to treat himself, let alone anyone else. Also he felt there was no real future in the job. He didn't want to be a waiter for the rest of his life. He had assumed this estate agency wasn't interested in him but they had been very busy and were just slow in responding to his application. Anyway last week they offered him an interview and he agreed to see them today as he knew he was off. The problem was that two days ago Asmodeus had come inside him permanently and as each day passed it was more and more dominating. It had ceased to be fun anymore and Peter really wasn't himself at all. He was beginning to get scared that he would lose his independent thought and Asmodeus would take him over completely. It really hadn't helped that his interviewer had been a very attractive young lady. Peter couldn't keep his mind on the interview and had to ask her to repeat a question several times. He knew he wouldn't get the job.

He had started his journey back to Brighton and had chosen the A259 coast road. As he drove he made up his mind to go and see Aleister today, before it was too late, while he could still make his own decisions. The A259 is a very hilly winding road and he had to keep careful concentration. He passed over the top of the South Downs near Beachy Head and down into West Dean. The road then climbed back up, passed the fish pond on the left by the old church and then weaved between the trees until the road started back down to Seven Sisters. As he passed over the single lane bridge in the Seven Sisters valley over the Cuckmere river, Peter's mind went back to the time when he discussed Asmodeus with Aleister. Aleister had said Asmodeus wasn't a problem, the demon hated water and if they immersed Peter in water Asmodeus would be forced to leave him and go back to where he came from. 'When I get back I'll go and see Aleister and insist he does that for me' Peter thought.

He drove up the hill and into Seaford town. As he came through the town he passed the turn off signposted to Wychamton where Carrie's cottage was. He didn't really think of her as Hecate yet and was very sad he couldn't call in and see her. No one wanted Peter to visit them because of Asmodeus. Peter couldn't understand that he had invited this demon and he couldn't believe it was all his fault. He had to see Aleister today and resolve this. Send this thing back, it was no longer fun, it was no longer a joke. It was destroying him. He had passed through Seaford now and was going back down hill towards Newhaven. As he drove down the hill, the sea was on his left and the big bay opened out showing the corner of the white chalk cliffs. He reached the bottom of the hill and drove over the railway bridge. Going straight ahead he then passed the bridge control hut on the left and drove slowly over the lifting bridge over the river. Turning into the one way system he saw the pub the Green Man and on impulse turned into their car park.

He walked into the pub, it was dim inside, caused by the heavy wood panelled walls and the weak lighting, but they had a real fire in the grate and it was warm and from the smile of the landlord, friendly as well. Asmodeus didn't try to restrict him drinking alcohol so was happy enough about the interlude. Peter did however worry that Asmodeus would like Peter's loss of control if he drank too much, which would make him particularly vulnerable to Asmodeus' domination. However after that interview Peter needed a decent drink, so ordered a double scotch on the rocks. 'Very poignant the rocks bit', he thought. It went down very well so he ordered another. After half an hour and two double scotches Peter thought he should make a move. However he wasn't keen on walking straight to the car in case an overly enthusiastic policeman was watching the pub car park and right now anyone would smell the whisky on his breath. Anyhow he decided he would like a walk, so he decided to stroll towards the river.

The lifting bridge was down and cars were slowly moving across the bridge. There was a footpath on each side of the bridge so he started to make his way across, on the seaward side. It was cold but there was no wind so it was not uncomfortable to walk. He got halfway across the bridge and stopped to admire the amazing statue of a cormorant that someone had fixed to the top of a post in the middle of the river. It looked so real. Then Peter's mind went back to Aleister's words about Asmodeus; how Aleister could send Asmodeus back to where he came from by immersing Peter in water. Peter was depressed and at the end of his tether. He needed relief from this dam demon. Peter was a very strong swimmer so wasn't afraid of water even if it was cold or tidal, but he was becoming afraid of this demon and what it was going to do to him.

Without any further thought Peter climbed up onto the metal box fencing that run along the side of the walkway. He stood on the top of the fencing swaying and looking into the water and then just jumped forward into the air. He took a large lungful of air a fraction of a second before he plunged feet first into the river. The water was freezing and nearly took all his breath away but he managed to continue to hold his breath. The tide was going out so there was a strong current pulling him along as he swam for the surface. Then he suddenly felt Asmodeus leave him and he felt a great relief that it had worked. He could see in the murky water below him, an outline that he assumed was Asmodeus. Then just when he thought he had won, a hand that felt more like a claw grabbed his ankle and started to pull him down. As he was dragged down into the depth of that cold fast running water, the blackness began to surround him. Bubbles began to escape from his lips as water filled his nose and mouth. He held his breath and kicked against the demon that clung onto his ankle, but his breath began to fail. Peter realised that the demon wasn't trying to save itself, it was vindictively murdering him. In his head he cried out to the Gods, but he knew he had renounced them all, in favour of Satan. But he also knew Satan wasn't going to save him. As he lost the battle, he called to Eostra and Jesus to forgive him, as his body convulsed and freezing water poured into his lungs. He was already becoming numb from the cold, but as he died he thought he heard the demon laughing.

Peter had lost the job that he loved, then the girlfriend that he loved, so he had become severely depressed and had also been drinking heavily on the day in question. The police investigation concluded that Peter had committed suicide.

Due to the police investigation and the post mortem, the cremation couldn't be held for nearly four weeks. Also due to the rumours about Peter being a member of a Satanic coven, no church would officiate the funeral or allow burial on their consecrated grounds. It was wet and windy on the day of the cremation. Peter's mother was still alive but in an EMI (Elderly Mentally Impaired) home, so couldn't come. Peter once said to Sue that he had visited her but his mother didn't know who he was. Therefore, there were only a few friends paying their respects. When Steve and Liz walked into the crematorium, they recognised Sue, his ex-girlfriend and her new boyfriend, Cathy (Liz's friend), Lauren and Carrie. There were three young people from the café where Peter had worked. There were also two other young people that Steve and Liz didn't recognise, maybe they had worked with Peter at the Estate Agency. Steve had agreed to do the eulogy. It wasn't hard to write. Peter was a good person who had had some bad luck and because of depression and desperation he had allowed himself to be led down a path he would not normally have considered. There wasn't an evil bone in Peter's body and yet circumstances had resulted in him joining a Satanic coven. It was a terrible waste of a young life. It was however, a blessing his mother had no idea, it would have destroyed her.

*The Famous Cormorant at Newhaven,
the sculpture is by Christian Funnell.

EPILOGUE

Steve and Liz were very happy with each-other and they had agreed that Liz should stop taking the birth control pill. They had made several decisions: to get married and love each-other until death, to move into Steve's house in Polegate, to have a baby before Steve is too old to play catch with his child, to name the child Peter if he was a boy, and to start a movement to bring together all the Pagan covens and take co-ordinated action against the evil of all Satanic covens. That would be the real eulogy for Peter.

****

Printed in Great Britain
by Amazon